WELCOME TO STONE CREEK

Lia Jensen

Contents

16 year old O'Connor Steele used to be a top notch Barrel racer until a freak accident which stopped her career. Her horse was put down and she was almost paralyzed in her left arm shoulder to hand.

Eventually she did get back in the saddle. Physical Therapy helped her regain full use of her left arm and hand. She hasn't barrel raced since. Instead she competes in hunter jumper and Cross country. Her parents and her chose out a new horse named Running Wind, a hot headed bay thoroughbred gelding that barely listens to her. When she and her Twin brother Adam get Accepted into the prestige Stone Creek Riding Academy she happily goes.

She is good in school but until she can over come her fears and make it through the year will she only feel complete. She uncover secrets some good some bad and some can save her from falling away. Drama doesn't help either. Boys come in to play friends stay by her side and she tries to make it through her sophomore year without getting kicked around by the populars' of the school. This is a story about trust, friends, hope and just a little bitta love.

Chapter 1

I leaned my head against the window the trees blurring the gaps filled with wide open plains with horses grazing.

"You know what, Connor I'm thinking of trying barrel racing. You think you can teach me?" I rolled my eyes at my brother knew perfectly well how to barrel race

"Adam," My dad warned from the front seat I stopped him before he could continue,

"Dad, it's fine he's being my twin brother" my Dad grunted but stayed quiet when my mom put a hand on his arm, "how much farther are we from Stone Creek?" We'd left a good two hours ago on our way to Stone Creek Riding Academy. Me and my Twin brother had been accepted after a whole summer of anticipation. We both have a horse that's a jumper but does rodeo skills to.

"Yep it's right up the road," I lifted my head up and saw large gates coming up on a gravel rode. We turned onto the road leading to the gates and I heard the insights welcoming us from the horses out grazing. My eyes widened in awe as the academy came into view. The minute the car stopped I'd already unbuckled and jumped out of the car only to slam into someone on my way to the trailer. My head collided with someone's shoulder and I ended up going back and slamming into someone else,

"Gee sis I know ya love me but I thought we talked about body slamming me" in return I elbowed him and stepped to the side looking at who I'd slammed into. He was a pretty tall guy.

"Sorry didn't see you there I'm O'Connor but you can call me Connor" I said a little awkwardly, any girl could see that this guy was hot - Dark brown somewhat long hair and forget me not green eyes - I offered my hand and the guy took it saying,

"That's fine, I was actually coming to see if you guys needed any help because I've already gotten settled. Oh and I'm Nick," I smiled and my brother answered before I could,

"That'd be great and what this midget forgot to mention is that I'm her Twin brother Adam" he offered his hand just as I elbowed him when he called me my ridiculous nickname that he gave me when we were little. Nick shook his hand and I started leading the way to the back of the trailer. I took off my baseball cap that said Equestrian across the top and stuffed it in my back pocket. I unlocked the trailer and saw my brother take a step back when Nick didn't I said,

"Your gonna want to step back" he did as I said and I swung the door open quickly getting out of the way just as Wind burst out, "You got him?" I yelled at my brother but Wind had already burst away and was galloping around the courtyard. I burst away and saw out of the corner of my eye Adam and Nick do the same.

"You guys block the entrances, he's gonna try to get away!" They did as I said and I grabbed the lead role as it came flying by me. I yanked it as Wind reared and dragged his face down to mine.

"Shh boy no one's gonna hurt you. Shh, come on let's go. For once he didn't argue and I led him back to the trailer the boys were following behind and Adam jogged up next to me.

"Ya got him from here?" I nodded and Adam ran off to get his horse Ceasar a warmblood gelding. Nick came up next to me after Adam left and let out a whistle,

"That's a hell of a horse what breed is he? And where in the world did you manage to find him?" I nodded smiling a bit,

"He's a thoroughbred and I saved him from kill buyers at an auction" Nicks eyes widened and he let out a low whistle,

"Well it's a good thing you were there because Its be mighty sad to loose a horse like this. Do you know what stable your in?" I nodded smiling a bit more,

"Yeah I'm down at stable six well thank you very much for helping me out but I'd better get going and make sure my brother doesn't get himself lost, I guess I'll see you around" I walked away and heard Nick call out behind me,

"I think you will I'm in Dorm six and barn six" I waved at him as I walked away and made my way to the trailer. After I tied Wind up, and started unloading his tack. I placed it next to the trolley that was filled up with my bags.

"Adam we need to go get checked in" he poked his head out of the trailer and came out carrying bulky western saddle,

"Kay just give me a minute" he put the saddle down on top of his English saddle and bridle, "Alright let's go" I nodded but before we left our parents stopped us.

"Alright you guys once we get you into your dorms we're gonna head out and while you get your identification were gonna stay with your horses" we nodded and left quickly going and entering the building. I walked up to the table that said six as we walked in and said,

"Hi is this where we check in for dorm six?" The lady nodded and said,

"Yep it sure is, I'm Josie the counsellor for that building and the Cross Country course instructor as well as the barrel racing instructor. Now then what are your guys names?" She smiled at us and offered us her hand which each of us shook,

"Its nice to meet you Josie I'm O'Connor Steele and this my brother Adam," I said introducing ourselves. She went through a few papers and pulled two out and gave them to us including a card and three keys for each of us,

"Alright then it's nice to meet you, here's your registration papers, student ID card and your three keys one to your dorm, dorm building and stable locker now then O'Connor it seems your roommate Casey is here and Adam your roommate Nick is also here. So you guys are actually the last ones arriving today the last three are arriving tomorrow so I can show you to your dorm and stable. Now then if you'll follow me" she said getting up and leading us out. We made your way over to the trailer where we introduced her to our horses,

"That trouble maker is Wind and the calm one is Caesar" Adam said pointing them out. Josie nodded suggested we grab our things and follow her to our dorms. Our Mom helped me with my stuff while our Dad helped Adam.

All I could say when we walked into the dorm was,

"Wow" There was a small kitchen in the corner with an island and dark grey granite countertops. The cabinets looked like a dark oak and there was about six stools surrounding the island. Then off to the side there was a large table with two benches on each side. I turned around and saw a living room on the other side with a large couch, loveseat and a large comfy chair that could fit two people. The part that completed it was the flat screen tv above the fire place.

My brother nodded his agreement and Josie spoke snapping me out of my daze,

"Ok so all girls are on the second floor and the boys are on the third floor. On Friday we usually have movie nights with popcorn and different snacks. There'll a total of eight students in our building. We're one of the smaller buildings because the others have twelve in each dorm. I'll explain the rest to you later but for now do you think that you boys can find your way to the third floor your in room number 2." Adam nodded and he and our Dad made their way up the stairs carrying the trolley between them.

"Now then O'Connor, Mrs. Steele if you'll follow me up Stairs. Anything I can do to help get stuff upstairs?"

"Nope I think we're good oh and I forgot to tell you earlier please call me Connor" Josie smiled,

"Alright then Connor up the stairs we go" Me and my Mom took an end each of the trolley and made our way to the second floor. By the time we made it up Josie was standing in the hallway with a tall girl with dark brown shoulder length hair and bright blue eyes.

"Connor this is your roommate Casey and Casey this is Connor," Josie said introducing us. I set down my end of the trolley and my mom made sure it was up straight. I stuck out my hand and shook hands with Casey smiling,

"Hi, it's nice to meet you Casey, I look forward to getting to know you" Casey smiled,

"Same here, well I assume we're not staying in the hallway so let's get you settled" I laughed and knew immediately that I liked her.

"Yeah and I bet your mom standing in the hallway would like to make sure that your dad and brother don't destroy his new room already" I Laughed at my Mom and went to drag my stuff into my room. My mom brought the rest in as I took in the sights of my room,

There was another room attached to the main Room with two closets as well as a shower and a bathroom with two sinks in it. The main room had forest green walls a loft bed with a desk under it with a cork board on the wall above it on each side of the room. There was a large shelf in the corners of the rooms opposite of the beds.

Me and my mom worked quickly pinning up posters fixing my bed sheets and putting my books in place on the shelf. I just finished pining up my last poster of a horse jumping on a cross country course when I heard a knock on the door.

"Can we enter the ladies domain without losing a limb?" I turned and saw my brother poking his head in my dad not far behind. Casey who was sitting at her desk reading let out a laugh,

"Yep I think so though Adam try not to destroy my room please" now it was his turn to laugh,

"Geez didn't mom tell you we did a good job on my room" I shook my head and they both walked in,

"Oh right Casey this is my twin brother Adam don't worry he's not all doofus" my dad came over and gave me a hug. He kissed the top of my head just as our mom hugged Adam and gave him a kiss and then they swapped repeating themselves with their other kid except my dad didn't kiss my brother,

"All right then kiddos, we're gonna head on out Josie had someone bring your tack in and Wind and Caesar are waiting for you guys when we walk out." I nodded and we all walked out as my parents said bye to Casey, who decided to come along and meet our horses.

By the time we made it out Wind was prancing impatiently at the trailer. I untied his lead and gave my parents another hug and Adam soon joined making one big group hug.

My Mom waved bye from the truck as they pulled away.

"Now are you gonna introduce me to this boy or what?"

Chapter 2

I turned to Casey as my parents pulled out of view,

"Oh this troublemaker, this is Running Wind otherwise known as Wind. Oh and watch out he's as hot headed as any boy especially since he's only three," Casey laughed and went up to Winds side and patted his shoulder. Oh, shoot,

"Casey watch out!" Wind reared front legs lashing Casey moved out of the way just as Wind's lead untied, I cursed under my breath and ran forward grabbing the lead. He reared again. Yanking the lead with such force that is threw me off balance. I looked up and he started coming down, someone grabbed me and dragged me out of the way as Adam ran forward and grabbed the lead yanking him down and started doing tee touch on his forehead which calmed him down by a lot.

"Hey you ok?" I stood up brushing myself off and turned around to see Nick standing behind me. I smiled,

"Yeah thanks a lot" he shrugged and Casey ran at me and gave a hug,

"Oh my god Connor I'm so sorry! I didn't think that would happen," I laughed at Casey's worrying,

"Hey it's fine with should've warned you that Wind is really tense around new people and sometimes even old," She finally released me and nodded,

"Ok so who's this?" She said motioning to Nick,

"Oh this is Nick he's in our dorm, Nick this is Casey my roommate" Nick smiled and accepted Casey's hand when she offered it,

"Nice to meet you Casey" she smiled back at him,

"Right back at you Nick,"

"Well then I'm gonna go save Wind from my brother and get him settled in,"

"Oh is it alright if I come I want you to meet Camelot my horse" I nodded and jogged over to my brother taking the lead from him. He gave me a pat on the shoulder then jogged off to get Caesar.

Casey fell in step besides me as we entered the stable, and again all I could say was,

"Wow" I led Wind over to the stall with his silver nameplate first one of the left just like home. Instead of putting him inside I tied his lead rope to one of the rails, planning on taking him for a short ride so he could stretch his legs.

"Ok so where's this Camelot?" I said looking around as Casey led me over to a stall that held a palomino,

"This is Camelot he's a cross between thoroughbred and quarter horse. I've had him about 5 years now" she said stroking him fondly,

"Well he definitely is a looker" she let out a snort,

"Compared to your boy over there I don't think so" I jumped when I felt my brother come up and put an arm around my shoulder,

"Aww thanks Casey I think I don't look half bad either," I elbowed him in the ribs,

"She was talking about Wind" he placed a hand on his chest acting offended,

"So there's a cafe a little while out that you can take a back trail on if you guys want to go on a ride," I looked over at Nick who I hadn't even noticed was there,

"Ooh that sounds great what's the cafe called?" This time Casey spoke,

"Ooh I know it isn't it the Harts & Hooves cafe?" Nick nodded and I unlatched myself from my brother.

"Ok so it looks like our parents set up our barn lockers so I'm gonna go get a bridle and ride wind bareback and I'll meet you guys outside" they all nodded and Casey joined me as I went to the lockers seeing as the boys were already tacked up planning on going. I opened my barn locker and grabbed my western bridle but froze when I saw the saddle on the bottom. I ran my hand over the saddle remembering the way it felt. It was my western saddle the one I haven't used since the accident. Shaking myself out of my daze I slammed the locker door closed and looked over to see Casey only have a bridle,

"I think I'll join you riding bareback." I nodded and led the way out of the locker rooms. We split up to get our horses. I entered Winds stall and slipped the bit in his mouth and the bridle over his ears. Finishing the bridle I led him out and saw Casey waiting with Camelot,

"Hey Connor do you mind giving me a leg up?" I shook my head and went over after tying Wind up I cupped my hands and she put her foot there and I boosted her up. As soon as she was up I jogged over to Wind and vaulted up turning to a Casey who was grinning,

"You need to teach me how to do that" I laughed,

"Ok I'll make sure I do" we kicked our horses into a walk and the boys joined us once we were out of the barn. I looked at Nicks horse who was a large warmblood and grey like Caesar but darker on his legs, face and tail,

"Who this guy?" Nick looked over and even though Wind was 17 hands high and Nicks horse a good hand shorter I was still shorter than Nick. Which was easy since he was like six foot and I was 5'4.

"This is Dante, I've had him for five years ever since he was two" I nodded and brought Wind over closer giving Dante a pat. Wind snorted at being so close to Dante and pranced throwing his head up I quickly turned him away and shot an apologetic look to Nick and trotted up next to Casey. Camelot seemed like the only horse besides Caesar that Wind got along with easily,

"So what are you specializing in? I'm doing dressage and show jumping," Casey said scratching Camelots

"Cool if I did dressage let's just say I would probably be dead last. I'm doing Cross Country and Show jumping," she nodded,

"That makes sense Wind looks like a jumper, um do you suppose that Logs supposed to be there" I looked up ahead and sure enough there was a fallen tree across the path. I pulled Wind to a halt which he fought but eventually gave but kept prancing I looked behind us at the boys,

"You guys ok to jump that?" They both nodded so I kicked Wind into a canter hopping for once he'd listen, he started to speed up but I kept a firm grip. I moved with him then gave him more reign and he pushed off, I went with him. He made it over the tree with ease and thankfully stopped on the other side when I asked. I moved him off to the side and turned around facing the others. Casey went over next, then Nick and finally Adam, I turned Wind around again and waited for Casey or Nick to take the lead it ended up with Adam next to Casey and me next to Nick.

"So how long have you had Wind?" I Looked at Nick then back to Winds head,

"About six months we got him six months after we had to put down my other horse Dancing Fire" he nodded understanding,

"So I heard when you and Casey were talking that you plan on doing Cross Country, might I wish you good luck Cross Country is the most competitive riding we have here besides barrel racing" looked at him quickly,

"They have barrel racing here?" He nodded,

"Down in arena 8 they just added it last year not many people do it because of how dangerous and competitive it is. It's one of the only ones that's not a class and you do in your free time" my eyes widened and then I turned to glaring daggers at the back of my brothers head, that explained the western saddle,

"Do you plan on doing it? I think I might try it out even though I'm not that good" looked back at Nick,

"No I used to but I don't anymore" clearly the look in my grey eyes explained I didn't want to be pushed about it,

"Do you think maybe you could give me some tips sometime soon? Like I said I'm not very good" I nodded and looked ahead again the cafe wasn't that far now and apparently Casey and Adam were racing as the path widened,I turned to Nick

"See you there" with that I kicked Wind into a gallop, this was the one thing he wouldn't try and stop he loved the thrill of a race. Heard Dante's hooves behind us but soon they got farther behind as we neared the other. Casey looked behind her and saw me her eyes widening in shock as we passed her and Adam. I tried to slow Wind down but he kept going, I gave a final yank and he stopped throwing me off but I was laughing as I lay on the ground and Wind stood there wondering where I went I stood up dusting myself off and went over to Wind throwing the reins over his head and tying him to the rail on the Cafe wall. The others were just tying their horses when I finished. I gave Wind a pat on his neck and kissed his nose, his fiery red coat glistened with sweat darkening his coat so it was darker, his legs were already black so they didn't darken anymore.

"Are you ok" I turned to Casey when she came up next to me and I nodded,

"Yeah it happens a lot Wind loves the run" she nodded and we made our way into the cafe followed by the boys.

. . .

I stared at the grilled cheese and Oreo milkshake in front of me. I took a sip of the milkshake and sighed at its cold oreoy goodness. Casey laughed at me from across the table sitting by Nick while my brother sat by me,

"So I take it you like it" I nodded and heard someone come up next to us,

"Connor its that you?" I looked up,

"Megan? Oh my god Megan!" I climbed out of my seat and gave her a hug, she was the same height as me with her blonde wavy/curly hair cut to shoulder length with warm brown eyes,

"Oh my god Connor I haven't seen you since well ya know! How are you?"

I smiled at her

"I'm good, oh right these are my friends Nick and Casey and you already know my brother" she nodded and we hugged again "pull up a chair and sit with us. What are you doing here?" She pulled up a chair and i sat back down next to my brother,

"Um I'm a student here what about you?"

"Oh my gosh me and Adam are students here too what dorm are you in?"

"Six I think is Dancing Fire here with you?"

"I'm in Dorm six to! Casey's my roommate, actually we all are and no Dancing fires gone. We had to put her down, but we have her daughter who we named Dancing Flames after her mom. I'm here with my new horse Running Wind he's the bay thoroughbred tied up outside," she turned and looked out the front window,

"Oh wow he's beautiful and I'm so sorry to hear about Dancing Fire she was an amazing horse"

"Yeah she was are you here with Claypso?" She nodded

"Yeah she's in the barn though I walked here," I nodded, I probably would've kept rambling had Casey not spoken up,

"So Megan who's your roommate?" Megan turned and looked at Casey

"Oh her names Amy Hill," Casey nodded,

"Yeah she's supposed to be coming tomorrow weren't you?" Megan nodded

"Mixed up the dates and came a day early" we all nodded and Nick spoke,

"So Megan where do you know Connor from?"

"Oh me and her did tons of circuits together you guys have got to see her ride she's amazing" Nick nodded,

"Yea we saw her clear a tree with two feet to spare on our way here,"

Megan laughed and I busied my self with eating the rest of my grilled cheese and drinking my milkshake,

"Jumping? Oh heck to the no I mean barrel racing surely you guys have heard about the great O'Connor Steele!" I was suddenly very interested in my milkshake,

"Wait you mean to tell me you barrel raced!" I kept my head down as Casey spoke,

"Yeah, but I don't really want to talk about it," everyone shut their mouths recognizing a tone that said i didn't want to be pushed. Standing up I looked at Megan.

"We should probably head back and hey Megan if you want you can ride double with me so you don't have to walk back" she nodded and we all went outside after paying.

I gave Casey a leg up and vaulted onto Wind while I held him steady Megan vaulted up after me,

"Hey so if you guys go this way it gets you back quicker" we all turned our horses and kicked them into a canter.

Megan was right it did get us back quicker but we still got back around 8:30.

"Ok you guys," we'd all finished putting our horses away and meeting Megan's horse Calypso, "I think I'm gonna head up to bed," Josie had asked us to get up around eight so we can help get the people coming tomorrow get settled. After we all said goodnight everyone followed in suit and went to bed.

By the time I took a shower changed into my pjs-shorts and a tank top- it was already ten. I crashed in my bed and Casey finished up doing the same I looked at the picture on my nightstand of me and Dancing Fire and whispered so quietly I almost didn't realize I'd said anything,

"Good night my fire I miss you" I turned off my lamp and snuggled into my blanket falling into a deep sleep.

Chapter 3

"Connor time to get up! Connor" I threw an uppercut at the voice trying to wake me up. I heard a grunt then a thud, "Really Connor! Geez now I know why your brother sent me to wake you up," I rolled over and opened one eye and saw Nick sitting on the floor rubbing his cheek.

I jumped out of bed just realizing I was in a loft bed and fell out of the loft onto Nick. I quickly scrambled off of him and helped him up apologizing over and over again,

"I'm so sorry,it's usually my brother who wakes me up and I always punch him because he wakes me up way to early. I'm so sorry, Are you ok?" He laughed,

"Don't worry I've been punched before but this is the first time for waking some one up." I smiled,

"Oh, well how'd you get in here anyways?"

"Casey let me in," I looked at her bed and sure enough it was empty, "She tried to wake you up earlier but to no avail so she asked your brother who made the excuse that he was eating breakfast so he volunteered me, probably because he knew that would happen," I grinned sheepishly,

"Yeah well thanks for waking me up anyways I'll see you downstairs in 7," he nodded and exited the room. Once he left I sank to the floor leaning against the bed frame and slapped my forehead,

"Nice way to make friends" I stood up and went to my closet in the bathroom, I pulled out my boots, jeans, black spaghetti strap tank top and my short sleeve Jean button up which I left unbuttoned. I looked in the mirror, and my reflection stared back, cinnamon blonde hair, not many curves but instead muscle replaced that. I pulled a brush through my hair, I threw it in a braid the short part of my frame falling out. Last thing for my ensemble I put on my cap and deemed myself presentable.

By the time I made it down the stairs everyone already here was eating breakfast in the living room watching random Tv. I grabbed a muffin from the counter before I walked over to them and sat down next to Casey. I stole the remote from her which was greatly protested by the others,

"Hold on I got a good show we can watch" I flipped channels till I found it and everyone calmed down when they realized the show was Heartland. I quickly finished my muffin and stood up,

"I'll be at the barn" they all nodded and I jogged out over to the barn. I fed Wind and the other horses for everybody and went to my locker. I opened it and the Western Saddle sat there in front of me, maybe if I just rode one round. . .

I quickly cleared my head and grabbed my cross country saddle and bridle along with my vest. I disposed of my stuff by the cross ties and jogged off to get wind. I slipped on his black halter and clipped on his matching lead on and lead him over to the cross ties.

I clipped him into the cross ties and grabbed my grooming kit. I quickly groomed him and gave him carrot. I hefted the saddle pad and saddle onto his back and slipped on my vest, I quickly led him from the cross ties guiding him with the reins. I walked him outside, threw the reins over his head and mounted up. Clicking him into a walk then kissing him into a canter and we went out onto the trails. I could see Winds breath clouding around his nose as we cantered down the trail and decided when his coat started to get damp to head back.

Before we left I pulled him to a halt and breathed in the fresh air the cold making my cheeks red. This was when I felt at peace. On a trail with wind in the fresh air. I kicked him into a gallop this time and by the time we got there the other students were already arriving. I pulled him into a walk, I guided him through the horses and horse trailers. I pulled him t to a halt about half way through the courtyard and jumped off finding it easier to guide him that way. We were almost at the barn when I ran into a girl leading a large light chestnut gelding.

"Really look at what you did now I can't wear this!" I looked at her curiously as she motioned to her hot pink ruffled top, nothing seemed wrong, "The whole front is wrinkled!" Well that's odd?

"Uh Sorry now if you'll excuse me" I stepped past her and Wind followed. Suddenly as we passed the large gelding he swerved and hit Wind with his rump. Oh boy this wasn't going to be good. Wind reared and so did the chestnut both started lashing out and I saw the chestnuts hoof collide with Winds side. The girl stood their frozen and the two geldings fought and moved toward her. I jumped into action, I ran at wind and the other gelding and grabbed their lead and reins yanking with all my might. A boy around my age came up and helped along with another boy. The first one took hold of Wind but Wind thrashed even more so I yelled at him,

"Get the other gelding under control I've got him" the boy nodded understanding an decent to help his friend with the other gelding. The girl just stood there until I yelled at her,

"What the hell are you doing get your Damn horse under control" as soon as my attention went to her Wind pulled with mighty strength yanking the reins out of my hands with such force that I fell backwards fast and hit the trailer behind me. I heard people yelling and the teachers finally showed up. I saw was Wind lashing out at anyone who came near me till they finally got him under control and the two boys from earlier came over to me and I took a deep breath regaining air and my vision cleared and I understood what they were saying,

"Are you ok?" I nodded my head and sat up wincing a little from soreness in my shoulders,

"Yeah I'm fine" I said and took the hand that the one with the darker hair was offering, "thanks and if you'll excuse me I've gotta go to my horse," they grabbed my arms when I tried to,

"Uh that's not a good idea the teachers said to stay away while they got him back under control" I stayed where I was and the same girl from earlier came rushing up to the darker haired boy and hugged him,

"Oh Will I was so scared Jake tried to kill me!" I looked at the lighter haired boy and raised my eyebrows he shrugged and said,

"Don't ask me and I'm Ben by the way and that's Will and Sonia who might you be?" I smiled,

"I'm O'Connor but please call me Connor thanks for your guys help but I think I better help the teachers before Wind kills some-one," just as I tried to sneak away Sonia turned on me glaring,

"Your the one who's horse tried to kill mine" I ignored her and kept walking, "that horse should be killed! He's psyco!" That's it. I turned and marched up right in her face and grabbed the front of her shirt glad that both the boys were standing back,

"What'd you say about my horse? I dare you to say it again" I said holding my fist up, ready to punch her until Ben dragged me back yelling,

"Don't say another thing about my horse! Stay away from him You hear!" I yanked myself out of Ben's grip and jogged over to where the teachers were trying to hold him. I saw one take out a tranq gun and I sprinted over to him. The teachers yelled at me to stop but I just ignored the and walked up to Wind who kept trying to rear. An audience had gathered but I ignored them and grabbed Winds bridle after shrugging off my Jean shirt. I pulled his head down to mine and put the shirt over his eyes whispering,

"Its just you and me now Wind" I mentally thanked the teachers for letting him go and saw out of the corner of my eye my Dorm arrive and my brother ran up to us slowing before he came near and stroked Wind on his neck.

"They want you to see if you can get him into his stall," he whispered in my ear and I nodded and started leading wind away and the crowd parted. I kept the shirt over his eyes until I got to his stall I took it off and led him into his stall. I took off his saddle and bridle and went out of the stall. Smiling when I heard him nickered for me for the first time. My mom always liked to think horses were like people and just needed a reason to trust their rider. I put his saddle and bridle away in my locker pausing to look at the saddle. I cleared my head again, grabbed my grooming box and jogged back to Wind.

My dorm stood at the entrance of the barn along with Ben, Will who were leading two horses and a different girl who made her way over to a stall with her horse that said Shamrock on it. Casey spoke first

"This is Ben, Will and Amy with their horses Star, Dash, and Shamrock. Oh yeah and what the hell happened?!"

"Boys got jealous and decided fighting was the best way to decide who was better. I've already met Ben and Will they helped get the other horse under control and Ben kept me from beating someone to a pulp. But I haven't met Amy," Adam nodded, that made sense to him,

"Wind has always been temperamental and his rider to" I shrugged and finished grooming wind. I looked at the small bleeding cuts. I sighed, thank god they were small, and looked at Adam,

"Can you patch him up?" Adam nodded and slipped into his stall. As soon as I saw Adam start patching the scratches on Winds side I stepped away and introduced myself to Amy,

"Hi Amy I'm Connor it's nice to meet you" Amy smiled,

"Nice to meet you too Connor" everyone finally stopped asking questions and dispersed to say hi to their own horses, while Ben and Will put there's in their new stalls. I walked over to Casey and Camelot asking,

"when are cross country team placements? I was never told" Casey nodded,

"Cross country's today show jumping next week and everything else after that. Here I forgot to tell you Josie gave me your schedule for classes tomorrow when you were out" she handed me a folded paper which I took and read while Casey continued,

"I compared our schedules and we have bio, math and show jumping together" I nodded and continued reading,

Algebra 2

AP English

AP Human geo

Bio

Gym

Show Jumping

Cross country and other riding activities will be held after normal school hours.

Any questions go to student services. Classes start September 3rd Cross country try outs August 31st.

I folded it back up and stuck it in my back pocket,

"Well I'm getting even more physical activity with gym right before show jumping" I said frowning,

"Well that'll be fun and you have Bio with Nick too, English with Will and Adam, and gym and geometry with the others. Also almost all of us have show jumping too." I raised an eyebrow at her,

"And how exactly did you find this out?" Casey smiled sheepishly,

"Umm we compared your schedule while you were out," I nodded and went over to where Ben was settling in his horse, Star from what the name plate said,

"So I think I owe you a thank you for keeping me from beating someone up on the first day" Ben turned around laughing,

"Hey it was no problem though just between me and you Sonia probably deserves it, has deserved it for three years,"

"Wow, I take it this isn't your first year," he Laughed,

"Yeah nope my first year was four years ago in sixth grade, me and Will have been coming here each year together roommates for five years now" I raised my eyebrows,

"Wow, you really have been here before, but anyways what's you story with this guy?" I asked Patting star on the nose,

"Ahh well let's see, I got him my eighth grade year so three years ago and well I've had him ever since. Bought him at an auction and well yeah that's it, he's a Belgian warmblood mixed with a thoroughbred, so what's your story with those boys over there?" He asked motioning to Wind and Adam,

"Hmm Wind well his show names Running Wind and he's a high strung Thoroughbred who I got six months after my old horse was put down, found him at an auction and saved him from kill buyers six months ago. And well now Adam hmm I've loved him for years and he loves me too and he's from my home town," Ben nodded seriously and I barely kept myself from laughing and when he looked at me I made my face very serious,

"Uh huh so he's your boyfriend or something," at that I lost it and started laughing,

"Nope I'd rather not date my twin brother" I looked at Ben in the eye being momentarily serious before we both lost it. Ben was the first to recover and I soon followed,

"Ok well if you don't mind me asking you have any guy in your life?" I shook my head,

"I've always been a single Pringle, right back at ya you got a special girl?" He also shook his head,

"Nope last girl friend was in eighth grade till beginning of my freshman year" I nodded, and Will walked up,

"So how's your horse doing?"

"Um my brother Adams patching him up I better go see how he is," I stepped away and jogged over to Winds stall and stepped inside next to Adam who was wiping off the small trickle of blood on Winds side which had stopped and there was now a small white gauze pad taped over the biggest area of scratches.

"How's this guy doing?" Adam looked at me,

"If what your asking is if he can be ridden in Cross Country placements today the answer is yes," I breathed out a sigh and gave my brother a quick hug thanking him before he left to check on Caesar.

I grabbed a sponge from my grooming kit which was right outside his stall, wet it with some of his water and got to work on cleaning the small amount of blood off his coat and for once instead of being tense with me around he visibly relaxed. I stopped wiping him and went to his head and whispered to him,

"We've gotta show them what you've got but in order to that you've gotta trust me boy just this once trust me"

Chapter 4

I slumped against my locker and slid to the floor and pulled my knees up to my chest. I leaned my head back and covered my face with my hands. I'd managed to keep it all in around everyone but here all alone I let it all come out. While I was trying to get wind under control the way he acted the way he attacked Jake and reared. My little Fire did the same thing and if brought back all the flashes I've been trying to avoid since the accident.

I heard someone come in and sit down next to me,

"I take it that you've got quite lot more going on than you let people see," I looked up and saw Megan sitting next to me. I nodded tears streaming down my face,

"The accident if was worse than you think" she nodded sadly and took me into a hug. We stayed like that for awhile until I raised my head,

"Ok I've gotta go get Wind ready for cross country placements," she nodded and we both stood up. I wiped my eyes and opened my locker grabbing my cross country saddle, bridle, saddle pad, and polo wraps which someone had slipped into my locker for me when Wind was getting patched up. I slipped my vest back on and made my way over to Wind dropping my stuff off at the cross ties. I grabbed Winds lead rope and quickly clipped it on him before I opened his stall door. I led him down to the cross ties and quickly re - groomed and tacked him. I led him to the arena that they said cross country was in and saw a few people already there including Sonia, Will, and Ben. I gave Ben and Will a small wave as I walked over. I pulled Wind to a stand still and vaulted up. I immediately noticed Wind was being extra tense and saw Sonia was on the gelding from earlier. I pulled Wind away and saw Ben come up next to me,

"So your a Cross country girl, I should've seen that coming especially with his build," I nodded,

"Yep I do Cross Country and Show jumping, what's your second riding expertise now that I see you clearly do Cross Country,"

He shrugged

"It's the only one you don't have to worry about how perfect you look and my second one is actually rodeo so yeah" my eyes widened ever so slightly,

"They have rodeo classes here" under my breath I added, "I'm gonna murder him" Ben looked at me curiously but nodded,

"Yeah they do Josie actually sometimes has us do rodeo skills to change things up a bit" my eyes widened even more,

"Well I might just pull a disappearing act on those days," his brows furrowed,

"If you don't know how, that's fine she usually uses some of the kids who have done it before as an example," I mentally sighed, I most definitely know how to do it,

"Um ok but anyways you ready for the test?" He nodded,

"I think so, oh and I forgot to ask how's this guy doing?" He said mentioning to Wind,

"He's gonna be ok just a few cuts" I heard a sharp laugh a little ways over. I looked over and saw Sonia laughing,

"Your just lucky that beast of a horse didn't kill Jake and that trick to calm him down, geez that must be one powerful sedative" my face hardened and I yelled at her back,

"If I remember correctly Jake's also the one who almost smashed you and if I hadn't yelled at you there'd be a Sonia pancake in the courtyard and your horse swung his rump at Wind not the other way around. So turn that petty little finger around because it should be pointing at you. And unless you want my fist to hit home this time I suggest you shut it," all the cross country kids stared at me and I saw Will choke back a laugh covering it with a cough. Sonia just gasped and Ben did the most ridiculous nothing he clapped and hollered,

"Get put in your place!" The rest of the kids stopped staring and laughed at Ben's comment until I heard a sharp whistle,

"Ok then Sonia no more comments like that because I'd really hate to break up a fist fight on the first day. Now then whose ready for some cross country?" Every body hollered,

"Me!!" Josie smiled,

"Alright then Connor your up first, the course is very direct so very little chance for you to get lost" I nodded and started out the arena. Once we were out I pushed Wind into a gallop slowing at the first jump and we cleared it! We kept a steady pace and I heard people start behind me. The last jump was coming up and we were halfway to it when Wind reared. I wasn't prepared but managed to hold on by grabbing his mane but straining my left shoulder while doing it. Wincing as I gathered the reins I continued the course. Just because it hurt didn't mean I couldn't still try my best. By the time I'd made it back my shoulder was throbbing painfully.

I saw Adam come out of the Arena Casey and Josie not far behind. Dismounting, I made my way to Adam, leaning against him, my limbs tired from the ride.

"Hey Connie what's happened? You took a lot longer than you usually do on a course," he asked worried,

"I strained my left shoulder a bit holding onto Winds Mane when he reared," I said tiredly,

"Alright let's go back to the dorms," I shook my head,

"I need to untack Wind," my brother shook his head as well,

"Nope, Casey's gonna do that for you," I looked back to see Casey leading Wind away.

"Fine," I started to walk but my brother swung me up into his arms, instead of protesting I automatically rested my head against his chest closing my eyes hearing him talk to Josie,

"She'll be ok she just needs some rest she always pushes herself to hard,"

"She seems like she's in good hands, I'll close up practice and let you guys go to the dorm without a fuss,"

"Thank you," as he started walking I buried myself deeper into his arms.

. . .

"Connor, Connor" I slowly fluttered my eyes open and saw Casey leaning down over me, I winced as I felt my shoulder throb and bolted up right,

"Fire!" I heard someone come running up to me and gently push me back down on my right shoulder making me realise I was in a tank top. I laid back down and pulled that blanket cover me over my left shoulder and saw it was my brother next to me and stroking my hair,

"Shh Connie it's ok it was just a dream it's ok" I blinked at him and started sitting up slower this time though and Adam helped me up. Someone had changed me into a tank and shorts. I felt my blanket fall off my shoulder again and kept my head down. I felt a few other pairs of eyes on me and saw Will, Ben, Casey, Amy, Megan and Nick all sitting down around me. We were in the living room on the first floor and the living room clock said it'd been three hours since the tryout.

Adam sat next to me on the couch and pulled the blanket back over my shoulder,

"You want your brace? You know the drill whenever you strain your shoulder," I nodded looking up. Megan was the first to speak after him,

"What happened?" I looked at her glad she wasn't asking about the two large scars that marred my left shoulder,

"Wind got spooked and reared, I almost fell off but managed to stay on by holding onto his mane but straining my shoulder in the meantime." Adam was gone about three minutes before he came back with a black shoulder brace. He helped me slip it on and I relaxed a little at the familiar feeling on my shoulder. While he was gone it had stayed silent.

"Did Wind get settled in alright?" I asked Casey,

"He was a little tense but he was eating and drinking water" I nodded and Will looked at Ben,

"Are you gonna tell her or what?" Ben shrugged and Will sighed just as Casey said,

"You two better spill" so Ben did,

"So Josie told us who got on which team and well you, me, Will, Nick, Sonia, Ally and Lukas made the advanced team and the other seven made intermediate," I gasped,

"But I barely finished the test!" Ben shrugged,

"Exactly what Sonia said but Josie said if you'd have finished without wind rearing you would've had the best time she's seen in years" I stared and Adam let out a whoop,

"And wait a minute Nick you tried out?" I said raising an eyebrow at his he shrugged while Casey grinned and said,

"It's a Friday and y'all know what that means," we all laughed and yelled

"Pizza!" With Adam yelling a lone popcorn. Laughing I scooted over on the couch for Casey and Adam to join me, while Adam started rambling,

"This calls for epic transformers movie celebration" everyone else agreed and congratulated me, Will, Ben and Nick on making the team. Adam turned on Transformers age of extinction and we all settled in. Amy and Megan ended up of the love seat, while the three boys argued who gets floor and who gets chair. That ended in all the girls telling them to shut up and sit down. Well mainly me and we just spent the night eating pizza, candy and popcorn and watching movies

Chapter 5

"Connor! Get up! You've gotta get up now!" I jolted awake at Casey's tone and quickly climbed down to her level,

"What's wrong?!" She smiled,

"Which top should I wear?" She said holding up a lavender blouse and a loose navy blue blouse, I rolled my eyes,

"The blue one of course, why?" She smiled again,

"Because our dorm is going to a grill tonight" I rolled my eyes again,

"I'm not going to any grill tonight" Casey stuck out her bottom lip pouting,

"Please, it's karaoke night," I took a deep breath and said,

"Ok but no singing" Casey nodded jumping up and down squealing,

"This is going to be so much fun!" I rolled my eyes at her excitement and went to change into something till I had to change for tonight. I put on jeans, red converse, a black v-neck tee and strapped my brace over my shoulder wincing as I tightened it. I quickly French braided my hair and went down stairs for breakfast running into Will as I did.

I gritted my teeth as pain shot up my shoulder and backed up from Will,

"Sorry didn't see you there" Will laughed,

"Obviously, how's your shoulder feeling?"

"Um like I strained it" Will laughed again,

"Well then I guess I'll walk with you down to breakfast," this time I smiled,

"My hero" we both laughed and made our way down the remaining stairs,

"Ah sleeping beauty arrives, how's the shoulder feeling?" I glared at Adam but replied,

"It'll be better once I take a few pain killers" Adam nodded and pushed them toward me and a cup of orange juice. I swallowed the pills and orange juice, grabbed a pop tart and made my way out only to be stopped by Adam,

"Umm I hope your not planning on riding" I shrugged and weaved past him out the door. I jogged out to the stable and went up to Winds stall. He immediately came over to me and nudge my right shoulder as if to say, ' where have you been I missed you' I kissed him on the nose and gave him a hug.

"How do you feel about going for a small walk?" he nickered and I opened his stall door and climbed onto his back grimacing a little bit. I walked him into an arena and saw as soon as I entered knew it was arena eight. The barrels were set up in that triangle pattern and I saw Nick enter on Dante riding western. He looked up when he noticed me enter and walked Dante over,

"I thought your not supposed to ride?" I shrugged, "Well since your here mind giving me a few pointers?" I nodded,

"Show me what ya got," he nodded and walked over to the starting gate. He nodded at me and I nodded back he burst out of the gate. He made it around the barrel well but when he got to the second barrel he lifted his hands to high and took the turn to tight thoroughly knocking it over. He didn't phase but continued on but ended up doing the same thing with the third barrel. They ran back fast but it didn't help much, he brought Dante over next to Wind and said,

"Umm yeah I did something wrong" I laughed,

"Yeah not that bad just a few beginner mistakes, when you were going around the second and third barrel you acted like you were show jumping. Also don't tense up when your going around the Barrel you've gotta trust Dante because when you tense up he can tell and well that happens, so go ahead and take him around one more time," Nick nodded and went back to the starting gate.

They burst out of the gate going around the barrels cleanly, his time wasn't amazing but it was a definite improvement. I clapped as they trotted over and smiled at Nick,

"Thats' a much better run," he nodded,

"Yeah it definitely is what you told me really helped. Well I think I better un-tack him we've been out here a good few hours. I nodded,

"I'm gonna do a little work with Wind then head in, you going to the grill place tonight" he nodded,

"Yep I guess I'll see you there" I nodded,

"See ya later then" he nodded and dismounted walking Dante out. I turned Wind around and dismounted wincing slightly at my shoulder but it felt better from the pain meds. I left Wind there seeing the gate was closed and walked over to the barrels running a hand over them I walked the course I stopped as I went to the third barrel memories flooding back. My last competition before the accident

"And here she comes folks that horse she's riding lives up to her name just a blur of fire! And she's done it folks she's broke the Arena record she's going to the big leagues!"

I sink to the ground tears streaming down my face and I hear hooves come up behind me. I look up and see Wind standing right behind me. He bent down to my face nudging me and I reached up and stroked his muzzle. Giving him a small kiss I stood up wiping my eyes and took a deep breath. I took hold of his halter and led him away,

"So little miss dramatic is also a crybaby" I froze and slowly turned around. My eyes hardened when I saw her,

"Oh and the only reason you're on the advanced team is cause Josie feels sorry for you. The minute she sees how bad you really are she'll kick you off the team" She said smirking, I glared at her and walked away. I put Wind in his stall and brushed him down. I slipped off his halter and hung it up, my brain still racking all the possibilities of not getting kicked out and still beating Sonia up. I walked back to the dorm my blood still boiling from what Sonia said. When I walked in I saw Adam and Casey laughing at the island . They took one look at my face and immediately asked,

"What's wrong"

"Nothing, I'm just annoyed with Sonia that's all." They both nodded and Casey gave me a look that said ' we're not done talking' she stood up smiling,

"Now then though we've gotta go get ready so we'll see y'all in an hour" she linked elbows with me on my right arm and dragged me upstairs.

As soon as we were in our dorm room Casey texted someone grinning. I soon found out she'd texted Megan and Amy cause the showed up at our door clothes slung over their arms.

"Ok pink or purple?" Megan asked coming in she held up a pink dress with ruffles and a purple on with a tight waist and somewhat floaty skirt. We all immediately gave the unanimous got of purple making us all laugh. Casey turned to me

"what are you wearing?" I shrugged my shoulders,

"I dunno give me a minute" I went over to my closet thought for a moment before pulling out my hunter green Jean dress with a wide leather belt. I showed them my choice and Casey basically yelled,

"Hell yeah!" We all shushed her and quickly got dressed after helping Amy realize that yellow dresses are her color not red. Casey disappeared again and into our closets. She came out a minute later holding two pairs of cowboy boots and two cowboy hats. I glared at her,

"This better not be a western grill" she just grinned and handed me the pair she found in my closet. I silently swore to murder my brother for bringing them but reluctantly put on my worn boots and black cowboy hat. The other girls each had pointed toe boots-unlike my round toe-and lighter hats. I strapped on my shoulder brace and stood up showing my finished ensemble,

"Connor take your hair out of braids please" Casey said sweetly. I shook my head the next thing I knew Megan was tackling me,

"I'll hold her down! You get the hair!" Amy and Casey laughed but did as they were told. I glared at Megan when she got off me glad she was careful with my left shoulder.

"Ok you need to wear your hair down more often, girl those boys'll be fighting to sit next to you or may I say a certain boy Will want to sit next to you" I raised an eyebrow at her,

"Real subtle Casey real subtle" she shrugged and led the way out the door,

"Oh and Connor you look really at home in those boots and hat. You should wear them more often" I shrugged again and followed her out the door linking arms as we went down the stairs Megan and Amy right behind us.

As we made our way down I saw the boys waiting for us. Adam let out a low whistle looking at Casey and I shot a glare at him. The guys were also wearing boots and hats Adam and Ben were the only ones looking at home in their hats which didn't surprise me. I walked toward the boys and raised an eyebrow when they didn't follow,

"So unless you boys just want to stand here staring at us all night I suggest we get going" everybody nodded and followed me out the door into the van we were borrowing from the school to get there.

I ended up sitting in the middle row between Amy and Megan while the boys to the back and Adam drove with Casey as passenger.

. . .

The drive was about ten minutes before we pulled up to a small grill/bar. The minute we walked in we were hit with the smell of fried chicken, burgers, ribs and fries. We made our way over to a small table of eight where I ended up between Will and Adam with Casey on Adams other side while the others sat across from us.

"Alright folks who's ready to get this night started!" Everybody let out a loud "We Are" before the guy on the stage continued,

"Now then as most of you know it's Karaoke night and for those of you who haven't been before here's the rules. We choose two people at random and they must sing a country duet song with each other. Don't worry folks though you get to choose the song and we'll play the words on that screen there. So to start us off you two in the corner" Everybody turned to see a coupe sitting at the corner of the grill near the stage. The couple stood up and made there way to the stage.

I didn't know what song they were singing but It sounded familiar.

"Hey Connor you want some fries?" I turned to my brother who was holding a basket of fries and nodded, taking the fries.

"Young lady in the black hat and the gentleman on the right, next to her please come on up," I froze as a light beam was shone onto me and Adam. I glared at Casey who'd told me I wouldn't have to sing and slowly stood up, making my way to the stage with Adam. The man handed us each a microphone and said,

"What song do you two want?" I looked at Adam and he shrugged indicating I could choose. I thought for a moment before saying

"Meant to Be,"

The screen in the back lit up with the words, the music started, Adam started it off first,

"Baby, lay on back and relax, kick your pretty feet up on my dashNo need to go nowhere fast, let's enjoy right here where we at

Who knows where this road is supposed to lead

We got nothing but time

As long as you're right here next to me, everything's gonna be alright If it's meant to be, it'll be, it'll beBaby, just let it beIf it's meant to be, it'll be, it'll beBaby, just let it beSo, won't you ride with me, ride with me?See where this thing goesIf it's meant to be, it'll be, it'll beBaby, if it's meant to be"

I joined in when it got to my part and I felt a lot of people stare at me as I sang

"I don't mean to be so uptight, but my heart's been hurt a couple timesBy a couple guys that didn't treat me rightI ain't gon' lie, ain't gonna lie'Cause I'm tired of the fake love, show me what you're made ofBoy, make me believe"

Adam stood there looking like a proud Dad after I sang and our group looked at me bewildered. Yeah yeah I get it I don't have a terrible voice. I got it from my Mom...

"But hold up, girl, don't you know you're beautiful?And it's easy to see"

I turned to him as we sang the chorus smiling as we sang together.

"If it's meant to be, it'll be, it'll beBaby, just let it beIf it's meant to be, it'll be, it'll beBaby, just let it beSo, won't you ride with me, ride with me?See where this thing goesIf it's meant to be, it'll be, it'll beBaby, if it's meant to be

So, c'mon ride with me, ride with meSee where this thing goesSo, c'mon ride with me, ride with meBaby, if it's meant to be Maybe we doMaybe we don'tMaybe we willMaybe we won't But if it's meant to be, it'll be, it'll beBaby, just let it beIf it's meant to be, it'll be, it'll be (c'mon)Baby, just let it be (let's go)So, won't you ride with me, ride with me?See where this thing goesIf it's meant to be, it'll be, it'll beBaby, if it's meant to be If it's meant to be, it'll be, it'll beBaby, if it's meant to beIf it's meant to be, it'll be, it'll beBaby, if it's meant to be"

Me and Adam stood on the stage for a bit and I started laughing when he took my hand and we did a dramatic bow. Going to back to the table everyone stared at me like I'd grown another head,

"What," I asked brows furrowed,

"Nothing you just didn't tell us your voice was so pretty!" I laughed as I sat down at Megan's comment,

"Well if I did I'd sound conceited and I don't usually sing," they all laughed and we spent the rest of the night goofing off and them trying to make me sing again.

Chapter 6

It's been 2 months since we came to Stone Creek and 2 months since I started practicing Cross Country an hour after school every week day and an hour on Saturday mornings. It's been 1 1/2 months since Nick made the Barrel Racing team and 1 month since Will broke up with Sonia.

"Nice job Connor just remember to let him come up to you a little more ok" I nodded at Josie and pulled Wind over next to Will and Dash, "Alright guys good job today and for some exciting news we have our first qualifying Cross Country competition next weekend on Saturday against Cross Stream academy!" We all let out a whoop and I turned to Will,

"Is Cross stream like our biggest rival?" Will nodded and I turned my attention back to Josie,

"Now then I must choose team captain and team rankings by Friday so I want you all at your best this week" We all nodded and I heard Sonia talking,

"Daddy's bringing me this new horse that's sure to get me the team captain spot sure she isn't super pretty but she's fast and jumps well" I couldn't hear what Kaylee said back but it got me wondering what the horse would look like

"Now then everyone go on and give your horses a good rub down. They deserve it just as much as you guys deserve to get some rest" We all waved bye and dismounted. I walked Wind over to the cross ties next to Will and Ben's horses,

"You know Connor you should just give up now you know there's no way your going to be able to win a ribbon or anything at that competition" I turned around and raised an eyebrow at her,

"Are you sure about that because if I recall correctly at our last Competition I placed higher than you" Sonia still smirked,

"That was just a lucky run but this time you better hope you have a few tissues to wipe your eyes as I wipe the floor with you and your mule that you call a horse" This time I lost it only to be caught by someone before my fist connected with her face. I struggled against their arms but to avail,

"I'll tell you one more time Sonia you stay away from me and my horse because one day there's not gonna be anyone to stop me from beating you to a pulp!"

She turned sashayed away her mid back jet black curly hair swinging as she did.

"Can I let you go now and not risk you running after her" I turned my head and found that it was Will that kept me from punching her,

"I guess but I swear one day she's gonna get it" He nodded and let me go watching me carefully as I walked back to Wind. I quickly un-tacked him and brushed him down, I thought for a moment before deciding today was a good day to give him a bath. I led him out to the outdoor cross ties and hose. I grabbed soap and sponges from my locker freezing for a moment as usual when I saw the saddle. I slammed the locker shut and jogged back to Wind.

I soaped up the sponge and sprayed Wind down enough that his coat was thoroughly soaked and shiny. I set the hose down and started soaping him up focusing on his back when I felt someone come up and tickle my side. I instinctively threw the sponge at their face,

"Hey!" I turned around and started laughing when I saw Will with a sponge on his head and soap dripping down his hair. He took the sponge off which made his hair stick up all spiky and made me laugh harder. He grinned,

"So it's like that now is it?" He looked at him curiously wondering what he was going to do just as he went and grabbed for the hose. I was quicker and grabbed it first while he grabbed the soapy bucket. He dumped the bucket on me while I sprayed him with the hose. Seeing he was unarmed he went up behind me and wrapped me up in a hug lifting me off my feet and soaking me. I dropped the hose and it landed in an angle so it was aiming up into the air making it rain on us while Will spun me around.

He eventually put me down so I could turn off the hose and once I did. He leaned in towards me about to kiss me but I backed away,

"I'm sorry Will, I just . . . I'm not interested in getting into a relationship right now." He stepped back as well looking highly embarrassed and a little bit mad and sad.

"I understand," I smiled at him and finished drying Wind off as he walked away. He took that a lot better than I expected.

. . .

Two days had passed since Wil tried to kiss me. even though it had been awkward we were still kinda friends. Team position tryouts were today and the team was going to be skipping the last two classes of the day so I was sitting in bio tapping my foot and watching the clock as Mrs. Tailor spoke.

"Alright then class just a reminder Cross Country Advanced team you are going to the stable after this class so good luck!" She finished just as the bell rang and I grabbed my bag running out of the classroom and down the hall only to slam into Will on the way out. He laughed and helped me up because this time I'd fallen on my butt.

"I guess you better stop making a habit of that or people might think you really wanna see me every time you go somewhere," ok so he still liked me. Great.

"Come on I wanna get there early to warm Wind up and if you hurry we can warm Dash up to!" He laughed but gave in and ran along side me to the stable. We went straight to our horses stalls and quickly tacked them up. I walked with Will and his horse into the ring and heard a familiar voice

"Oh come on you stubborn thing!" I turned and saw Sonia struggling to get her new horse I figured into the ring. I froze when I saw the horse, the scars in the same spots the same chestnut coat and fiery eyes. I backed up slowly my eyes widened and Sonia saw me,

"Huh I guess all it took to break you was one look at my amazing new horse" the horse calmed down when it spotted me and just stood there staring her eyes never breaking mine even as she was lead into the ring.

I thought she was dead. I felt someone run up next to me as I fell to the ground kneeling.

"Connie what's wrong?" It was Adam.

"She's here" His eye's held question but I stood up before he could ask and walked into the arena my legs shaky but I felt Adam and Winds strong presence next to me and it was enough to get me through. Sonia smirked when she saw my face,

"Oh it's ok I hear the Intermediate team isn't that bad" my glare hardened on her mad that she was on that horse and that she was such an idiot. I nearly smiled,

"You know you have to get used to a horse before you take it out on a course and it's good to know that you'll have fun when your booted," She smirked,

"I have and yeah good luck at getting me booted" My gaze stayed harden as I mounted Wind and rode him around the ring warming him up. I pulled him up next to Will,Ben and their horses, Adam walking off to the side of the arena understanding dawning on his face just as Josie walked in,

"Alright folks so yes I know I told you team placements are today but the fact is I've already tested you and today I want to see your ability to do different kinds of riding and test your bond with your horse so I want you guys to do some rodeo skills today so I suggest you get a different saddle" We all stared but did as we were told except I froze as I stared at the Western saddle and bridle sitting in front of me. I took it and quickly changed winds saddle shaking as I tightened the girth and buckled the bridle on. I buckled on the martingale, running my hands over the familiar seams and creases of the saddle. The leather still smelled of rodeo and I smoothly mounted. Closing my eyes as I sat down.

I kicked Wind into a walk and made my way into the arena. No one else was in there besides the barrels set up in their familiar pattern, so I took a chance. I went in the starting gate taking a deep breath I kicked Wind into a gallop. I smiled at the feel of not having a helmet on and the wind blowing trough my hair. I brought him around the first barrel not taking it tight and the tension all falling away. I did the same with the second and third. the minute I turned around the third I Kicked him on we ran as fast as we could down the aisle only slowing down when we came up to the gate.

I pulled him to a halt and sat there hands shaking as I laid the reins on his neck and all I heard was the sound of our breathing. Then the silence was broken by a hand clap,

"Um Hey Connor why are you bothering with Cross Country when you can do that" I froze tensing up and quickly dismounted my legs threatening to buckle as I hit the ground. I turned to Josie my face stone,

"Because I gave that life up when I lost my other half" She looked confused as did Will who I found was also standing next to her. He gave me a sad look. I realized how it sounded so I continued.

"Because it's something I chose to leave behind Fire was my life and when I lost her I quit"

"Fire was your horse?" I laughed even though it wasn't a laughing matter,

"Yes she was my horse, my other half, my everything!" His face slowly turned a little red and he looked down ashamed. I walked over to Josie and Will, I trusted Will he was a good friend but not someone I had romantic feelings for. But being a good friend was good enough th for me I just didn't want to tell him yet. But I could tell Josie she proved I could trust her many times over. So Josie sent Will to finish tacking up Dash and I told her my story.

I told her about the accident and how I quit barrel racing and why my shoulder was so scarred because I had a very deep fracture from the accident and finally I told her the crazy part,

"That crazy horse Sonia has I think it's her it's my girl and my parents didn't really put her down". She nodded,

"I understand but there's not much I can do but I'll help when I can. Now though you've gotta get going before you really do get booted from the team and show off your mad Barrel racing skills" I shook my head,

"No one else can know but more importantly I'm not sure how Fire will react to the barrels. From the looks of it she's been retrained and hasn't ridden around the barrels since I rode her." Josie thought for a minute,

"I trust you so we'll keep a careful eye on her while she in the arena, if she gets out of hand I leave it to you," I smiled my thanks to her and we went into the arena. Mounting back up on Wind I thanked him for holding him for me.

"Alright Ben your up first if you don't know the barrel racing pattern let me know ok and you are being timed so give it your all" Ben nodded and went to the starting gate. Sonia was the second to last which was me and as she made her way to the starting gate my eye's never left the horse. Sonia nodded to open the gate and she was off, until she wasn't on the horse anymore. Fire reared hooves lashing as Sonia tried to bring her around the first barrel. She threw Sonia off and went back down only to start bolting and bucking around the arena. I jumped off wind and yelled at Josie,

"Get them out of here and let me do this PLEASE!" Josie nodded and herded the rest of the students out but stayed in near the gate as I ran to my Fire. Her eye's flashed recognition as I stood in front of her begging her to calm down. She came down onto all for hooves and we stood there as she pawed the ground and suddenly her eyes focused on something behind me. I turned around and saw Sonia knocked out on the ground holding a whip in her hand. I glared but turned my attention back to Fire,

"Ssh girl she's not gonna hurt you anymore it's just you and me now no one else" Fire lowered her head to my level and looked at me her eyes full of hurt and sorrow now and a little anger. I reached out and she pressed her cheek into my hand snorting breath. I took hold of her reins and led her out calling for Josie to help Sonia. Josie ran over to Sonia with Lukas the senior in our group following her. I led Fire out talking to her gently and stroking her neck. The team cleared the way as I led Fire through to the cross ties. I was just taking off her saddle when I heard Sonia yell,

"Don't bother with that horse she's going straight to a meat house Ya here don't bother" Good thing I never listen to Sonia. Instead of bringing her to stable one I put Fire in the empty stall next to Wind who I found Will had taken care of. I walked out of her stall in a daze and I felt Adam take me into a hug,

"I'm so sorry Connie, I swear I didn't know, what do you want to do next?" I backed up a little bit to look at him and said,

"Now I talk to out parents,"

Chapter 7

"Oh honey we're so sorry, you already in grief when she got hurt and we couldn't tell you she was gonna be alright especially after saying you were never gonna barrel race again. We never thought she'd show up at the school." My mom said crying my Dad at her side and Adam at mine as wee talked through Skype.

"I get it Mom but this time we've gotta take her home her riders selling her and I can't loose her again" my Mom nodded,

"We'll call her new owners" we waited a bit before they came back on screen, "she was already for sale and they happily finalized the deal, we're picking her up tomorrow," I nodded and after saying bye I closed my laptop, I leaned into my brother who embraced me.

"You aren't mad?" I shook my head,

"I understand why they did it doesn't mean I like it but I get it," I heard a knock on the door and left my brothers embrace to get it I was met with 5 how are you and one I'll punch Sonia for you from Nick. I smiled at my dorm touched that they cared. Accepting a hug from Casey I said,

"I'll be ok, I'm gonna go for a ride who wants to come," everyone said yes and we mad your way to the stable. By the time we got to the barn it had started to rain and from what we could see that rain was becoming snow. I jogged over to Winds stall and gave him a kiss on his nose. I froze when I heard laughing much worse. Sonias' laugh. Taking a deep breath I clipped Winds lead on and led him out of the stall to the cross ties. I clipped him in and smiled as he nudged me, the first time he'd ever done that. I smiled and threw my arms around his neck, breathing in his horsey scent I whispered so only he could hear,

"You are my only boy and I love you" he nickered and thrust his head against my chest as if saying 'I know' giving him another kiss on his nose I went into the locker room to get my saddle and froze when I heard Sonia's voice,

"O'Connor Steele right? Famous barrel racer then oh look at this a tragic accident and her Career ends" I turned around slowly to face her. She has a smirk on her face and her eyes are narrowed,

"I wondered whether it was true or not, I guess it is I wonder what the school will say to that. Better yet your friends." She walked forward face triumphant and I heard someone enter the stable I looked and saw Megan taking in the scene. Sonia not noticing continued,

"Who would've thought your just a little brat that gave up the minute she got a small scrape." I clenched my fists shaking in fury,

"And that horse I mean what types of owner does that to their horse," that was it. She pulled the last straw, launching myself at her hand balled in a fist I punched her straight in the face. Sonia stumbled back into the wall. I could hear Wind pawing the ground behind me his head going up and down as if to say,

"Oh yeah she deserved that," dang it. I looked at my hand already bruising and of course the smart me had punched her with my left arm. Well it was definitely gonna need ice. Looking back at Sonia I saw her clutching her eye,

"What the hell! The principal will hear about this." I glared at her,

"I'll tell you this once more and only once more, come anywhere near me or my horse and I'll punch you so hard that pretty little nose of yours breaks. Stay away from my friends horses and family as well. You got problems I can tell. But if you can't figure out those problems, then leave us out of them. Because either have never ever done anything to deserve this type of treatment from you," Sonia just gasped at me and I turned heel and marched back to Wind.

I was done fighting her, she needed to figure out her problems and not drag other people down into them. I took a deep breath as I picked up a soft brush and began finishing the grooming I'd started earlier. Murmuring soft words to Wind I calmed him down a bit. I finished grooming him and went to get my saddle but not before I felt a rush of dizziness. I saw Megan coming over with her horse. Seeing me leaning on the wall she rushed over,

"Connor? What's wrong?" I looked at her,

"I feel dizzy, really dizzy," she nodded and helped me sit down.

"Alright keep looking at me and take deep breaths your having a panic attack," I did as she said and saw her take out her phone, calling someone, she started to get blurry and I struggled to keep my eyes open,

"Hey Adam get down to the cross ties now. It's Connor, she's having a panic attack," I managed to stay conscious, and I hear someone else come up recognizing the voice as Nicks,

"Megan? What's going on?" People constantly seem to be asking that today,

"She's having a panic attack, would you try to calm Wind down he's freaking out," I heard faint bobbing and the jangling of lead ropes. Megan started to get blurry again,

"Connor no! You are not allowed to pass out! You hear me!" I heard a large neigh, and a thud, Megan's faced was replaced by Wind's and I saw Nick coming after him rubbing his butt,

"Damn horse got away as soon as I tried to take him to his stall," smiling a little I gathered some strength and rested my hand on Wind's nose which was down and sniffing me.

"Good boy Wind," starting to breathe easier I heard Adam's voice,

"Connie!" I felt him start pulling me into his arms.

"Come on your going to the nurse." Like I usually do when I'm in Adams arms I snuggled deeper into them and laid my head against his chest.

"Nick, can you take care of Wind? Megan can you find Josie?" I heard each of them agree and take off doing their assigned jobs. Adam started walking,

"Ahh Connie what are we going to do with you?" I smiled at him a bit and closed my eyes no longer able to keep them open. Adam would keep me safe. My brother always kept me safe.

Alrighty I'm gonna change it up a bit and put it in Nicks view so we know what's going on while Connors asleep.

"Come on Wind, you can't follow her," it was amazing how protective he'd become of Connor in just these past almost three months. Connor definitely one who's to work her magic. I struggled with the high strung Thoroughbred for about 5 more minutes before he finally went into his stall and started to quite obviously mope around.

Making my way out of the stable I jogged to the nurses building only to see the rest of my dorm making there way as well, Casey in the lead.

Slowing down I started walking next to Casey,

"Nick, so you know what happened?" She asked,

"Yeah she had a panic attack not sure what from though," Casey nodded,

"I think I do," I gave a confused look but she didn't say anything else.

When we got to the nurses office the front desk lady looked a little over whelmed with us all there so me and Casey had the others go sit down and we spoke with the front desk lady,

"We're here to see Connor," the lady looked in her database,

"Room 6" we thanked her and mad your way there. The building was a little to much like a hospital and it kind a freaked me out. There were maybe three other students occupying the rooms

"Alright then Connor your on a strict resting policy, no school or riding for at least two days," we all smiled a little when we heard Connor start protesting on the no riding policy but the doctor muscle shushed her. Poking our heads in the room we saw Adam, Megan and Josie standing the right of Connor the nurse to the left.

"Surprise" We all said smiling when we saw Connor sitting up looking much better than when we saw her in the barn.

Chapter 8

Connor

"Hey guys!" I smiled at the rest of my dorm and let out and oof as Casey tackled me into a hug, and then punched me in my right arm,

"Your not allowed to have panic attacks dummy! You almost gave me one!" I laughed,

"Sorry it wasn't something I planned on," smiling I swung my legs over the side of my bed as I was about to stand Adam beat me to it smiling at the doctor as he picked me up,

"Don't worry doc I won't let her do anything but eat and rest for two days," the nurse started laughing as my brother carried me out of the room with me slapping his chest and our dorm following. He carried me into my room and probably would've tucked me into bed in my dirty riding clothes but I made him put me down so I could shower and change.

Once I finished my hot shower I pulled on sweats and a tank top enjoying the feel of comfort. Leaving my bathroom I saw everyone had left finally. Slipping into my bed my eyelids fell shut and I fell into a deep relaxing sleep.

...

I opened my eyes sun leaked through the blinds giving the room a sunny glow. Slowly I sat up yawning and wincing from the stiffness in my back.

"Your awake!" I looked over by the Windows and saw Megan jump out of Casey's desk chair. Nodding I slowly climbed down my ladder yawning. Rubbing my eyes I grabbed my zip up hoodie from my desk chair and slipped it on. As soon as I had it on Megan wrapped me in a hug,

"We were so worried!" I let her hug me for a minute longer before pulling way,

"Not that I don't love you or anything it's just I love food more and my stomach is calling for some."

Megan laughed,

"Better be you've been asleep for a day and a half!" My eyes widened, that meant I had four days to get ready for the competition against cross creek. Running into my bathroom I yelled behind me to Megan,

"I need to take a shower, make me breakfast pretty please!" I heard laughter and the door of my dorm room click shut as I turned on the shower and got in.

By the time I was dressed in riding pants, boots, a plain black long sleeve work out shirt and braided my hair it was 1:00 pm running out of the bathroom I raced out of the dorm and slammed into a chest. I really needed to stop doing that, I looked up from where I had fallen on the ground and saw Nick looking back at me green eyes twinkling with laughter,

"Need a hand up there sleeping beauty" rolling my eyes I took the hand he offered and he pulled me up so we were standing chest to chest faces inches apart,

"Connor I . . . I was sent to tell you your breakfast awaits" I smiled and nodded my stomach growling its thanks. sidestepping him I continued on down the stairs and smiled when I saw everyone at our table. I was nearly in heaven when I smelled bacon and waffles, I more like floated over to the table and sat down in between Casey and Will with Adam on Casey's other side.

Digging in I ate more then anybody else and finished earlier,

"I going to the stable," nearly everyone said no in unison per usual,

"Yes" I said right back, "just cause I'm not captain on the cross country team it doesn't mean I'm not competing with them next week,"

"But aren't you still tired?" Adam reasoned, I shrugged

"Just a little I should be fine," he pursed his lips but nodded and I stood up. Nick stood up as well as Will who both said at the same time,

"I'll come," they both glared at each other so I looked to Casey for guidance but she just shrugged no help what so ever.

"See now I've got two grumpy Body guards, I'll be fine" leaving the table Will and Nick followed. I basically jumped on Wind when I saw him but I settled for hugging his neck. Nick came up next to me, Will was gone and getting Dash,

"I exercised him for you yesterday, he was doing this weaving thing in his stall so I figured he had a lot of pent up energy," I nodded my thanks, "Adam should've told you this morning but he forgot, your parents came and took Fire home for you yesterday they were talking about retiring her since she's been through so much. I heard your parents on the phone say she seemed back to her old self when she got home," I smiled at that. At Least all that was taken care of. I looked at Nick finally noticing the dark purple bruise on his cheek,

"Nick what happened?" I asked pointing to the bruise he shrugged,

"Whacked myself with a saddle tacking Dante up," I frowned but didn't press turning back to Wind I slipped his lead and halter on while Nick went to get Dante. Leading him to the cross ties I clipped him in next to where Will was brushing Dash. He smiled when he caught me watching and walked over, giving me an awkward hug until he realized I wasn't returning it.. Looking up at his I saw his lips in a frown, backing up I said,

"I need to get Winds tack" pulling away I jogged into the locker room and headed straight to my locker. Opening it up I grabbed my cross country saddle, bridle, polo wraps, vest and grooming box. Hurrying back to Wind I groomed him quickly and saddle him up. By the time I was putting the polo wraps on Will and Nick were already warming up in the ring. Slipping off Winds Halter I slipped the bit into his mouth and bridle over his ears. Leading him to the arena I vaulted up and kicked him into a trot sighing slightly at the familiarity.

In the light of the arena I got a clearer look at Will and Nicks' faces. My lips tightened into a straight line when I saw a bruise on Nicks cheekbone and Wills' jaw. Pulling Wind to a stop in front of them the looks on their faces told me everything I needed to know.

"You two need to pull your heads out of your butts and learn to get along. I have no clue what that fight was about but I don't care get it together. Your on a team together for God's sake." They lowered their heads not meeting my gaze, shaking my head I kicked Wind into a gallop out of the arena toward the cross country course. Why the heck do I have to have the craziest of days?

I slowed Wind down to a steady lope towards the first jump and we sailed over it. At least our relationship had improved over the past few months. I know I should probably be worried that my parents took Fire home without me but I'm not, they took a load of my chest and at least fire was with flame - her daughter - now.

Taking a deep breath as we neared a bush jump I slowed Wind down a bit and he took the jump with at least 6' to spare. We continued on just me and him wind rushing past us. Smiling I kicked him on faster as we neared a him and stood in my stirrups leaning forward. He went up the hill in lengthy strides. I looked to the side and saw a rabbit dart out of the under brush. Not good. Wind reared but I stayed on and turned him in a tight circle when he landed keeping him from doing it again.

Patting his neck I whispered calm words, as soon as he stopped quivering I kicked him on back toward the stable.

By the time we got there the sun was starting to set and it was starting to drizzle. I dismounted and led Wind over to the cross ties where I'd left my grooming box. Unsinching winds saddle I slid it off of him and set it down next to my grooming box. I slid his bridle of and slid on his halter. Clipping him into the cross ties I grabbed my curry comb and started rubbing it across his back in smooth circles where the dirt from the course had made it onto him. I put the curry comb down and grabbed my hard brush. Wind shifted and snorted at someone. I looked up and saw Will standing at his head and rubbing his nose. I stood up ignoring him and started brushing wind again till all the dirt was off and his coat was clean. Taking my soft brush just as Will started to talk,

"I'm an idiot and I'm sorry Nick was just being a jerk about you being hurt and it made me mad," I looked at him, that didn't sound like Nick but people change. I nodded and continued brushing Wind till his coat was sleek and shiny. Will came up behind me,

"I'm really sorry Connor," I rolled my eyes,

"It's not me you should be apologizing too and besides I'm not your keeper I have no say in who you fight. All I'm saying is that we're supposed to be a team, me Nick and you so just put aside your problems and get along. 'kay?" I heard Wil mumble an ok and walk away.

Chapter 9

"Connor. . . Cccoooonnnnnnnnnnoooooorrrrrr."

"Go away!" I swatted my hand at Casey's voice and heard her laugh,

"Up and atem your two days of no school are up! Meaning I'm no longer alone in most of my classes!!" I laughed and opened my eyes finally. Casey stood on my ladder dressed in a flannel and jeans,

"Best part, it snowed on the last week of school before break!" I sat up quickly, riding in snow was always fun with Wind,

"Really?" She nodded and jumped off my ladder so I could get down. Climbing quickly I ran to the window and saw a beautiful layer of snow coating campus. I smiled and ran into my closet getting dressed quickly similar to Casey in a blue flannel and worn jeans. Pulling on my cozy winter boots I stood up and brushed my hair not bothering to put it up I pulled on a beanie and vest.

Standing hands on my hips I smiled at Casey,

"I'm ready for school!" Casey laughed and grabbed her bag as I grabbed mine. We made our way down the stairs arms linked and laughing. Each of us grabbing a muffin off the counter we ran outside into the snow laughing.

I stopped in the middle of the court yard and looked up into the sky opening my mouth for the snowflakes to fall into. I heard Casey snicker and felt two arms encircle me from behind. I squealed as they lifted me up and swung me around. Out of the corner of my eye I saw Adam swinging Casey around. When the world finally stopped spinning my spinner and me fell to the ground. I gasped as the cold seeped into my pants and jumped laughing. I turned back to my spinner and saw Nick lying on the ground laughing. Offering him my hand he took it and as he started to get up I let go and he fell back on his butt. Snickering I adjusted my backpack and walked over to where Casey had ran off from Adam linking arms again we waved our hands at them and continued on towards school.

Soon after we left the boys Wills voice danced around in my head,

"Nick was being a jerk about you being hurt" the smile dropped from my face and I frowned. I shook my head and took a deep breath, the smile resumed on my face and I looked at Casey,

"Race ya," I took off running through the snow Casey yelling and laughing behind me as she started running. By the time we made it to the school our cheeks were red and we were breathless. Linking arms again we made our way to math. As we walked into class I felt people's eyes on me but I didn't question it I was the girl that got in a fight with Sonia then I heard a hoot and holler,

"Connor you finally decided to come to class now did you!" I rolled my eyes at Ben and we made our way over to the back row where he was. I sat down next to him and Casey on my other side. Noticing we had a few minutes till the bell rang I started talking with her about what I'd missed in my classes luckily not much just mainly studying for finals on the next three days.

It was a minute till the bell rang when Adam and Will walked in. Adam looked like he wanted to punch someone and Will looked no better. Oh boy. This wasn't going to be good. Adam made a bee line for the seat next to Casey and sat down heavily Casey grabbed his hand and squeezed it. Me and her were going to be having a talk that's for sure.

Will took the seat next to Ben and sat down just as heavily. What the heck was going on with the Boys today?

"Alright class . . ." I tried to pay attention to Mr. White but my thoughts kept distracting me. Why the heck did guys have to be so complicated. Take a deep breath I spent the rest of school trying to focus.

By the time Cross Country practice came around I was exhausted. Show jumping had been canceled due to our instructor being sick and wanting to give us the day off so I ran back the dorm and quickly changed in to riding pants, a dark red long sleeve work out shirt and a grey fleece for Cross country.

Grabbing my helmet and I ran to the stable when I got there no one was there yet so I quickly tacked Wind up and brought him to the arena when I got there I was surprised to find Josie with the beginner show jumping team still,

Josie looked over when she saw me and called me over,

"Perfect just the person I needed to see," I gave a confused look,

"Would you mind mounting up? I need a favor," I nodded and vaulted onto Wind earning a couple oohs from the younger team. I kicked Wind into a walk over to Josie, and she held his reins for a second so she could talk to me,

"I'm helping them go over the course but I can't really show them right now since my horse is stuck on stall rest due to losing a shoe and we can't get a new shoe till the snow melts. So can you go over the combinations for me? It's be a huge help!" I nodded,

"Sure seems simple enough" and the highest jump was maybe 2" not even. Kicking Wind into a canter when Josie let go of his reins she explained to the team I was gonna show them how to do it. I loped Wind around a bit to warm him up and directed him to the course. Counting the strides in my head we came up to the first jump and made it over easily same as the next eight jumps. Pulling Wind to a halt next to Josie the team applauded me and Josie smiled,

"And this my munchkins," I snickered at Josies name for the younger kids, "is why Connors captain of the Advanced Cross country team" I gasped,

"B-b-but I thought you chose someone else," Josie smiled

"Now why would I do that?" I gasped at her,

"Why me?" Josie smiled softer,

"Your a leader, a great rider and I've never seen someone love horses or riding as much as you do," I smiled shyly,

"Thank you Josie, I won't let you down, I promise" Josie laughed

"Good cuz I plan on winning," I laughed and waved bye to Josie and her young team.

As soon as we were clear of the stable I kicked Wind into a gallop towards the trail near the Cross Country course as soon as we were on it I let Wind loose and he took off his mane billowing into my face. Smiling I let go of the reins and clutched his mane instead. I let him keep running like that till I glimpsed the sun setting and realized he'd shown down showing we'd been riding for awhile. Looking at my watch I mentally slapped myself. It was almost four which meant we had only a few minutes to get back to the stable for practice. Turning Wind around we took off and Wind seeming to know we needed to hurry ran as fast as he could.

By the time we got there Josie had just begun practice and everybody was warming up. Wind pulled on the brakes right before we bowled into Josie who started laughing. Apparently she was talking about me,

"And well here she is guys your new team captain!" Everyone was clapping and laughing until I heard a familiar shrill voice,

"What!?! Her!?!?! You pick her to be our team captain!" Josie spun around to face Sonia who I now noticed was sporting a black eye.

"Yes I did now if you have a problem with it I can just as easily boot you down to intermediate as easily as I can boot someone else up!"

Sonia shut up at that and I realized that she was back on Jake the rude gelding that fought with Wind our second day here.

"Now Connor I want you to start practice today better yet I want you to run practice" my eyes widened,

"Don't worry I'll still be helping and coaching I just want you to come up with what we're going to practice today" I nodded,

"Okay then I guess... How about we start with partner runs, I want you guys to team up and try to match pace with each other and go over the wider jumps so you can get to now each others speeds better or the way you ride," Sonia snorted,

"So you want me to keep pace with these slow people?" I shot her a glare,

"No I want you to keep pace with me." Someone snickered, I looked over and saw it was Nick,

"Your in for the ride of your life Sonia," I smiled at him,

"Alright I'm going to try and pair you up the best I can, let's do Ally and Will, Lukas and Ben then first ones back can decide who's going to pair with Nick. Go only as far as the Bush jump which will give us about 3 or four wide jumps," Wind started to prance under me from standing still for so long so I turned him in a tight circle,

"Ok what are we waiting for? Ally, Will your up first" the took off keeping pretty good pace though Will was a little ahead. I nodded to Lukas and Ben to go next then me and Sonia lined up, I smiled at her while she sneered,

"I'm not holding back so your job is to keep pace with me. Got it?" She rolled her eyes and nodded. We took off I pushed Wind and

I could already hear Jake's shortness for breath I pulled Wind back for the first jump and so we were keeping better pace with Jake. We continued on like this and though I hated to admit it if there was reversing a thing of parter pace cross country we'd be quite good at it. We finally soared over the last jump and i smiled at Sonia.

"You still think you can keep up?" I kicked Wind into a Gallop and Sonia did the same with Jake we raced back streaking across the field. As the Stable came into view we raced to it the gate was open so quits was in the stable. I pulled ahead by at least three tail lengths and beat them. Smiling snarkily as Sonia and Jake came to a halt Sonia glared at me,

"You cheated!" I heard a laugh and saw Ben and Star standing near by with their partner Lukas who was also laughing,

"Sonia Wind had already gone a sprint just a little bit ago so even if she had cheated there's no way she could have won if her horse was slow," Sonia clenched her jaw and kicked Jake into a walk over to the corner. Going over to Ben I gave him a high five,

"Thank you for that," Ben shrugged,

"It was the truth," just then the last pair came bolting in. I recognized the horses first, this wasn't going to be good they were almost dead even but the grey one had pulled ahead of the brown one first. It was Dante and Dash, really not good cuz that meant it was Will and Nick.

"I won!" Will discounting a fist in the air, uh oh,

"In your dreams I pulled ahead Blondie," Nick said, I moved myself and Wind in between them first,

"You fight right now and I'll kill you both myself." They both shut up,

"Will go by Ben Nick go by Ally" the both nodded, turning to everybody I smiled,

"Good job today everybody your looking Sharp I think you and your horses definitely deserve a good rest. Go give them each a good rub down and throw on their blankets tonight it's supposed to get cold. Now get out of here!" Everyone except Sonia laughed and dismounted, leading their horses to their own barns.

I dismounted off of Wind and made my way over to Josie who was beaming.

"That was great Connor, you handle the team well it helps a lot that you also seem to know each of their personalities, weaknesses as well as strengths," I grinned,

"Thanks"

"Now I'm going to give you your own advice, get out of here!" Laughing I dismounted off of Wind and led him away smiling widely.

Chapter 10

I officially love weekends and hate getting up early even if it's for a show. The school week ended quickly with the fact being I'd only been in school for two days and now it was the day of the show. My alarm had gone off at 3 am due to the fact it was a four hour drive and we had to be there and ready to ride at 8 am. Yawning, I slid down my ladder and pulled on my white breeches, a pair of black sweats over them and a grey athletic long sleeve with thumb wholes deciding to change into my nice black one there and avoiding the chances of it getting dirty.

Packing my athletic jacket, cross country vest, black helmet, paddocks boots and black half-chaps into my duffel I pulled on my moccasins and also hunter green SCRA cross country team sweatshirt. Before leaving I Dragged a brush through my hair leaving it down and put on my equestrian ball cap. Slipping out of my room I closed the door so I wouldn't wake Casey and made my way out of the dorm. Yawning as I walking into the Cold air and to the barn I took a deep breath of the warm horse and hay smell filled barn.

Making my way over to Wind I stepped into his stall and patted his neck waking him up. I'd seen Will, Ben and Nick already in their horses stalls but I didn't bother going over to them. Pulling on his leather halter I clipped on his black lead line and led him out of the stall to the cross ties. Clipping him in I picked his hooves and groomed him quickly before pulling his blanket back on and slipping his hooves into his travel boots. Although I'd groomed him the day before Wind has a special talent of getting dirty even with his blanket on.

I stepped back and thought for a second before I put his tail in his tail bag not wanting it to get super tangled before the competition. Leaving him there I went and grabbed my all-purpose saddle and bridle, before i changed my mind I grabbed his Martingale and black saddle blanket. I walked quickly over to him just in time to see Josie show up with Ally, Sonia and Lukas with their horses along with Ben, Will and Nick at the cross ties brushing their own horses. Smiling at them all I set my saddle down next to where Wind was patiently waiting head bowed down dozing. Patting his cheek I turned to Josie,

"We heading out yet?" She nodded her head,

"I'm choosing which cars you go in and which trailers your horses go in. Oh, and Casey and Adam are coming as well I decided they would come for the experience and because Adam said and I quote, "I wanna see my little sis kick all their butts and sass them into oblivion," we all laughed and I smiled,

"Lead the way then" taking Winds lead rope I hefted my duffel onto my shoulder and picked my saddle up with the same hand balancing

It on my forearm, bridle just barely off the ground in the same hand. As we walked Josie explained the seating arrangements to me,

"I've put you with Adam, Casey, Nick and Ben while Ally, Lukas, Sonia and Will are in the other car, horses are in the trailers that are attached to their riders car. I'm driving the car your in so someone is sitting up front with me and the others are having Lucy another dorm hall manager drive them." I nodded and led Wind into the trailer after giving Adam and Casey my stuff and respectfully punching Adam good morning.

"Alright guys I want Adam, Casey, Nick, Ben and Connor with me in the front car then the rest of you are are in the second one put your horses in the trailer attached to the car your in and let's hurry up and get this show on the road," I dropped off my bags and tack into the trunk and quickly led Wind to the front stall of the trailer and locked him in. Giving him a kiss on hiss cheek I ducked out of the stall to clear the way for the others. Sliding into the car I saw it was basically a mini limo with wrap around seats that each were a bit longer and wider than normal ones. Stealing the seat closest to the window Nick slid in on my left, Casey on my right Adam next to her and Ben took the front seat headphones on. I grabbed the throwbacks and pillow before settling with my head on the pillow on Casey's lap and my legs curled next to me.

Josie looked back and smiled,

"Alright guys try to get some shut eye during the drive." We all nodded and settled back as the drive began. Everyone fell asleep fairly quickly and I felt Nick lean over and whisper in my ear,

"You can stretch out onto me if you want" Nodding I stretched out my legs across his lap and fell into a deep sleep.

* * *

"Alright guys wakey wakey! We're here!" Everyone groaned and I yawned loudly and stretched. Connor you've trapped two people in come on get up," sitting up I remembered I'd stretched out over Nick and used Casey as a second pillow. Sliding out of the car the team ran to the trailers in search of their horses

Going through the side door I stood by Winds head and patted his neck waking him up from his nap. As soon as everyone else had their horses out I ducked out of the trailer. Sure Wind had been better about getting out of the trailer but the look in his eyes when he saw the people and horses around through the open door said enough luckily Ben had closed the trailer door behind him. I had already untied his lead so now was just to catch him as he came out. I looked around and spotting who I needed I called him over,

"I thought he was over this trailer craze?" Adam said, I shrugged back,

"New place, so many horses and people doesn't mix well with especially after that long of a ride. You should know this," now it was his turn to shrug, "you take the door I'll take catching him," Adam nodded and stood by the latch while I stood nearby to catch him.

Nodding Adam swung open the door and Wind came running. Lunging I just barely caught his lead rope as he bolted by and I heard a few gasps from the crowd. Then a whistle. I rolled my eyes an mumbled under my breath,

"You have got to be kidding me," pulling harder on Winds lead rope he kept rearing and I felt someone start pulling from behind me. As soon as he was down on all fours and taking a breather I vaulted onto his back lead rope in hand. I turned him in a tight circle and saw exactly who I thought had shown up to help. Jake Meiers, captain of the Cross stream cross country team who also happened to beat me in the last two competitions. Funny his name was the same as Sonia s rude gelding. Jumping off Wind as soon as he calmed down, I led him away and saw Adam and Casey had grabbed my tack and duffel bag. Casey came up and handed me my duffel,

"Me and Adam will take care of Wind and you can go get changed and get your number from Josie I think she said your last but she thinks Wind needs a good warm up" I grinned at her,

"I don't know what I'd do without you," I turned and made my way over to the bathrooms to change. I changed quickly my hands shaking like they did before every show as I braided my hair and put it in a bun and pulled the hair net over it. I slipped out of the stall and went over to the sink. Looking into the mirror I put my duffel on the ground and splashed my face with water hands shaking. Going to the towels I dried my hands and slid down against the wall eyes watering.

What the shell is wrong with me? I never get this emotional before a competition but it's just like last time. Fire was so high strung before the competition and I ignored her thinking she was excited. But where'd that get us? The barrel cut her and her tendon strained big time because I didn't listen. I heard the door open then close and I saw Sonia walk in. She slid down next to me and didn't say anything. Just sat with me. Eventually she did speak,

"I'm sorry. I know I'm terrible. I know I'm a brat. But you don't get it, I had it all, a boyfriend, and amazing horse, the best one at the school, and everyone liked me. But then you came along," I tried to cut her off but she held up her hand and continued,

"I know you never did anything to me, but just seeing you with everyone I felt like I lost my place. But I'm tired of being that bratty girl that's jealous of the new girl, I want to start over. But I don't know how. You've been through so much and I made it that much worse for you. I know you don't owe me anything but I was hoping. . . Maybe you could help me?" She looked at me tears streaming down her face and I realized she meant it every single word of it. Giving her a small smile I nodded,

"First lesson stand up," we stood up together facing each other, "don't act above anyone, act as their equal no matter who it is because no one's better or worse than someone we're all equal some of us just can't see that," taking her hand I picked up my duffel bag and led us out of the bathroom to the team.

"Guys gather up please," I said and they did just that their eyes widening at the shock that I was holding Sonia s hand and she was still crying.

"I want you guys to each look at each other. I know we don't get along most of the time and I know it's impossible to do so but we are a team and we stick together no matter what. Don't look down on each other look at each other as equals. Because that's what a team does. They work and listen to each other. Now what are we?!" For a second I thought they wouldn't answer then Sonia did and I repeated my self this time they all answered laughing as some of their voices cracked.

"Alright guys go get ready we got a show to win!"

Chapter 11

"Ok bud it's just gonna be you and me out there, and we're gonna show them what we can do," I said buckling his throat latch on his bridle smiling softly.

"You ready to go?" I heard Will say coming up next to me

"All ready, how'd you do?" He was still in his Cross Country vest so I could figure out he just finished his run.

"Not good, the course is tougher than it looks so be careful and try to keep Wind under control no matter how strong he is," I step back no longer smiling,

"Whats that supposed to mean?"

"Nothing but he's just strong and unlike some riders you can't always control him," now I was completely backed up my hand on Winds neck glaring,

"I think you should go check on Dash,"

"Connor I didn't mean it like that," he said, I turned around and started tightening the girth,

"Really then how did you mean it?" I said and felt him grab my wrist yanking me around,

"Just stop for a minute Connor! Your over reacting!" Now I was mad,

"You better walk away right now before we both say something we regret," I said glaring but Will didn't let go of my wrist instead his grip tightened, "Will, let go that hurts!"

"Connor would you calm down I didn't hurt you!" I kept tugging my wrist but he wouldn't give. I felt Wind start prancing, my eyes widened as I realized I hadn't tied his reins to the trailer yet.

"Will let me go, Win-" Will glared,

"No this is about us not Wind," Suddenly Wind was in between us snorting at Will pawing at the ground with his front right hoof. I walked to his side and started stroking his neck glaring at Will I took Winds reins,

"You better stay the hell away from me and my horse Will. Friends don't treat friends this way." Holy Crap that just happened.

Turning away I led Wind down to the starting gates my number just being called as third on deck. Taking a deep breath I wiped the tears that were coming yet again today.

Looking at my wrist my eyes widened at the bruises on it. Guess Will had a harder grip than I thought. Lining up I saw Adam and Casey coming over, shoot they saw the bruise and I'd be part of a murder, pulling on my black gloves I pulled my sleeve down over my wrist as much as I could.

"Hey sucker you ready to kick some butt out there?" I flashed Adam and Casey a smile seeing Adams arm around her waist.

"Did Will come and talk to you about the course?" I nodded frowning,

"Oh yeah he definitely did," Adam looked confused,

"What'd he say?"

"He told me I can't control Wind very well like other riders can and I needed to be careful," Adams hand that wasn't around Casey's waist was now in a fist,

"Now he's done it," I shook my head,

"Hes right though I can't control Wind,"

"Connor look at me," I looked up to see my brother looking at me with a soft gaze,

"You are the only rider Wind will listen to, when we exercised Wind for you Will tried but the only one Wind would listen to enough to actually move was me and Nick so we put Nick on him. The only reason Will said that was because he's jealous, jealous of the bond you have wind. Don't ever doubt that. Trust Wind out there, he trusts you now all that's left is to trust him," I wiped away the silent tears that had starting falling down my face,

"Thank you, now you wanna give me a leg up," I said reverting back to myself, he grinned and did as I asked. Sitting up on Winds back I took a deep breath and kicked him into a walk as they called my number. The last one. But I refuse to be the last one. I was going to be first.

"Alright boy let's show them what we got."

"Number 36 O'Connor Steele riding Running Wind,"

Kicking him into a gallop we were off running up the hill to the first jump. Leaning forward he took off his legs pumping like pistons underneath me. Slowing him down a bit we soared over the first jump. We landed, the first jump clear, then the next and the next and the next.

As we came up to the largest heel with a corner jump, I pushed him faster, it was the last jump, we could make it. Winds breath came in puffs the beat of his strides matching my heart beat as I slowed him to a fast canter as we approached the jump,

One two three, one two three.

His front hooves left the ground as did the rest of him stretching over the jump, me with him, smiling on his back. We were clear! He continued on and we crossed the finish line.

"O'Connor Steele riding Running Wind with the time of 12:06, putting her in 1st place by 1:02," I gasped and patted Winds neck,

"We did it bud! We did it! We're going to nationals!"

"Connor!" I looked up and saw everyone running over to me. Pulling Wind to a stop I dismounted him and have him a big kiss on his muzzle just as everyone reached me.

"You did it Connie!" I turned around just as Adam wrapped me in a big hug and spun me around. Laughing when he set me down the rest of the team tackled me in a hug besides Will who wasn't there and Sonia who stood off to the side, as though she was unsure of what to do. After everyone got off me I walked over to her and gave her a hug.

She was stiff as though she hadn't been hugged in a while but after a moment she melted into me returning the hug and whispered

"Thank you Connor," in my ear. Letting go I walked back over to Wind and saw Nick standing with him,

"Good job out there Connor," he said giving me Winds reins. I smiled at him,

"Thanks, looks like after break its gonna be even more chaotic." He nodded and walked away, after waving,over to Dante who stood patiently by the trailer to be groomed further.

Turning back to Wind I smiled at him,

"O'Connor Steele could we have a moment?" I turned around and saw the judges and announcers standing with them holding a medal. I nodded suddenly feeling very shy as I felt people's eyes watching me,

"Ms. Steele we should like to congratulate you on this win and we hope to see a performance as amazing as todays at nationals, " I smiled at them,

"Thank you very much and I can tell you that as long as I have my horse there will always be an amazing performance," the crowd chuckled and I accepted my ribbon that said,

"Finals winner, advancing to Nationals on it with the words Cross country and a jumping horse in the middle" as soon as the judges left I turned to Casey and Adam,

"Sooooo what now?" Adam laughed,

"Now you train for nationals," I smiled,

"You mean our team trains for nationals. You forget I put our whole team in first not just me,"

"Hey, Connor?" I turned around,

"I just wanted to let you know I've decided to leave Stone Creek and try again at home," Sonia said and I could see in her eyes its what she wanted, I nodded and gave her a hug,

"I hope you'll come visit" Sonia smiled, and whispered in my ear again,

"Thank you for everything," I smiled as we pulled apart,

"It's what any human wit morals would do," smiling she made her way over to two adults who looked like her parents.

"You did good Connie, you did good," I smiled at my brother.

"I actually think I did," walking over to the trailer I heard someone behind me,

"Seems like I'll be seeing you at Nationals O'Connor." I turned around to face Jake,

"It seems like you will. Hope you don't mind taking second place," he smirked,

"Not as much as I like first," i smirked as well,

"Well then that's too bad for because I mean that's what your getting now," I said pointing to the leader board that held the ranks. His face turned red as he marched away. Turning back to my friends they started laughing,

"You got some roasts in that brain of yours now don't you," I smiled at Lukas the source of the comment,

"You betcha," slipping Winds bridle off and halter on I tied him to the rail on the trailer and started untacking and grooming him. I didn't bother with the tail bag since the competition was over for today and put on his cooler instead of the blanket seeing how sweaty he was and how if we needed the trailer had a few heaters for the horses. I finished up with his travel boots and led him into the trailer. Ready to head home. When I came out I saw everyone grinning at me,

"What's up you guys?" Casey broke first,

"Me, you, Adam, Ben and Nick all get to stay an extra two days! I planned it before you left and packed you a bag." I raised an eyebrow, "Josie already talked to Sonia about her going home with her parents so she's gonna go back with them in that car leaving us with the other one since two of us know how to drive and on the way back we can trade off. A stable owed Josie a favor so the horses and trailer will stay there while we go to the town's winter festival! The one requirement from the stable is that we ride in the parade on the last day! Naturally we'll be riding western and of course we already said yes!" By the time she finished talking she was panting and I was smiling,

"Sounds great!" Grabbing my hand we tugged me out of the trailer and we closed it up getting ready to first go to the stable and then the hotel to drop off our stuff. As I was walking my tack into the trailer I realised that there were western saddles in there. Dang Casey really had planned this out. Making my way to the car I heard music coming from it and Josie talking to Adam through the driver window,

"Make sure you guys are on your way back Tuesday morning ok? That's when I told your parents that you'd be coming back. Now be safe, Casey and Ben are in charge," we all started complaining at that but Josie held up a hand a I got in the car,

"They planned it and they're not as hot tempered as the rest of you, now get going!" We all laughed and waved by to the rest of the team and drove to the stable. By the time we got there it was 6 and starting to get dark.

Unloading the horses and hitching the trailer took an hour, especially when Wind sprinted out of the trailer and I missed his lead. With the horses all tucked in Ben this time drove to the hotel and Casey got us checked in while Adam went in search of dinner. We made it to the room and I swear I was drooling at the sight of the fluffy bed. The one bed. Turning to Casey I grinned and dropped my bag inside the room,

"First one to the bed gets heavenly sleep!" I sprinted to the bed and Casey tackled me as I jumped on the bed. Laughing we laid on the bed coming to an agreement that we'd share,

"Can we come in without losing a limb?" We laughed at Adams voice and I replied,

"Depends, do you have food?" I heard some whispering before an answer,

"Yep! Fries for maladies," we laughed at the answer and got up to let them in. Once inside I grabbed the five guys bag that Adam held in his hand to find two burgers and two large fries. I looked up and saw Casey had two Oreo milkshakes in her hands from Nicks drink holder that now held only two drinks. Smiling I fist bumped my brother,

"You definitely know how to find good food." We all laughed and I handed Casey her burger and fries.

"Now out of the ladies domain,"

"Wha-" Adam started to protest but Nick put his hand on his shoulder and shook his head,

"Not worth it man, definitely not worth it," me and Casey giggled as they left the room Adam looking quite glum.

Casey and I stayed up till at least one in the morning just talking, and watching movies. I told her about what happened exactly between Will and I as well as, what happened with Sonia. By the time we passed out the streets were quiet and we were exhausted. Going to sleep for once I didn't dream.

Chapter 12

"Girls! Let's go already!" Casey and I laughed as the boys banged on the door.

"Just a minute it takes more than five minutes for ladies to get ready unlike you hooligans! Now go get us some food and we might consider coming out," Casey shouted, we heard grumbling and the sound of footsteps fading away.

"Dang, remind me to have you on call whenever Adams annoying me," Casey grinned and sat down in front of me done with the two Dutch braids she'd done for me,

"I actually have a huge favor to ask, would it be alright if I spent break with you? My parents are going to be in Alaska for all of break working on a rescue horse program but they won't be able to come home and I don't really want to spend break alone at the school," I grinned my eyes lighting up,

"Heck yeah that would be amazing!" Casey's whole face lit up,

"Great! Now lets finish getting dressed then then we need to go shopping for the parade, we are going to look amazing!" Casey said heading to the suitcases,

"Here wear this," she tossed me my form fitting black and grey flannel as well as jeans and a white long sleeve top to go under it. I smiled,

"You finally understand me," she laughed,

"I always did," grinning I went into the bathroom and changed when I came back out Casey was changed into a purple long sleeve shirt, fake fur lined fleece, jeans and winter boots. Casey tossed me my knitted beanie and vest,

"Your gonna want to wear those and those," she pointed to my winter boots, "it's hella cold," smiling I finished my ensemble and grabbed my phone and wallet,

"Lets go already I'm starving," we made out way out of the room making sure to grab the room key. Walking down the stairs to the dining area to find the boys at a booth with waffles on five plates. Slipping into the booth, me next to Ben and Nick and Casey next to Adam who pecked her on the cheek.

"Finally we can eat," Ben said digging into his waffles. Smiling I dug in as well not before I heard an annoying laugh,

"Wow I wouldn't have come here if I'd known it was the loser hotel." I looked up and saw Jar with his team,

"Great it really is the loser hotel now Jake, your here," I heard a snicker come from behind me,

"Yeah right Connor just wait till nationals, it's a full eventing competition, last I checked I'd never seen you do a dressage competition," I stood up,

"Just because you haven't seen me do it doesn't mean I can't. Besides," I smirked, "I've already proven I can beat you at jumping and that's already let's see two thirds of the competition," Jake's smile fell,

"We'll see Connor we'll see," I glared and sat down as he left. Everyone stared at me,

"You. Are. Crazy."I grinned at Casey,

"I know," laughing we finished eating, while the others grabbed their stuff Adam draped his arms over my shoulders as we walked out of the dining area,

"I didn't know that it was eventing did you?" I shook my head,

"We will be ready I trust my team," Adam looked at me seriously,

"You've lost two members of your team, two new members are coming in including two new students," I gave his a confused look, "Sonia s left the school and Will transferred to Jake's school and team," my jaw dropped, Will left?

"You didn't know did you?" I shook my head and his gaze softened, "Cross Stream offered him a scholarship after seeing his ride, can't say I'm sad to see him go though," I nodded and the others caught up,

"Now then, Connor and I will be going to the stores shopping for the parade outfits and you three will go and make sure we have all the tack and tack apparel for the horses then we'll meet up at 2 for a late lunch and early dinner. If your late no food because the parades at 4.

So make sure your dressed before then. You boys got that?" All of us nodded to Casey,

"Lets get to it then," I looked at the time 10 o'clock meaning we had 4 hours till we had to meet up at lunch. Catching a cab, the boys took the van, we headed downtown to the town's strip mall.

. . .

"How bout this?" I looked as Casey pulled out the millionth outfit. It's not that I hated shopping I just didn't love it either. This outfit was a grey and blue fitted flannel with, naturally, jeans and a pair of blue and black cowboy boots. This was the best one yet. We'd bought blue and black chaps at a different store as well as the boys outfits. Apparently they were each a size medium. How Casey knew this I have no clue. Which in my opinion is kinda scary.

"I think we have our outfit," Casey grinned and I grabbed the same clothes just in my size.

"Alright it's 1:45 so we need to go back to the hotel for lunch right after we check out," I nodded. While Casey checked out I waited outside the store and something caught my eye.

I pushed off from where I was leaning on the wall. Walking across the street I walked into the small tack store. Walking straight to the bridges I saw a black western bridle with a light blue design on the brow band. I looked at the price. Not cheap but I could afford it. Grabbing it I checked out and made my way over to where Casey was waiting,

"What'd you get?" She asked nodding to the bag in my hand,

"A bridle," she didn't ask any questions just nodded and waved down a taxi.

By the time we got back it was almost exactly 2. Making our way into the dining area I tossed the bag with the boys clothes at Adam.

"No complaining if it doesn't fit just suck in your gut." They all just blinked at me. "You heard me. Now let's hurry up and eat. I want to see my horse," they grinned,

"He's in the trailer the parade starts closer to the hotel so we figured that we'd just bring the horses with us," smiling I went over to the buffet and grabbed a grilled cheese and a fruit salad bowl. Jogging out of the hotel I ran over to the trailer and swung open the door heading straight to Wind. Who was, per usual, in the first stall. Weaving through the horses. I wrapped my arms around his neck breathing him in.

"I missed you boy, you miss me?" He nickered, settling down by his feet I started rang giving Wind the apples from my fruit salad.

"Connor?" I looked up to see Casey coming into the trailer already dressed for the parade,

"We need to get ready. Parade starts in an hour," I nodded and stood up,

"Alright then work your magic," smiling Casey grabbed my hand and pulled me the whole way to our room. Sitting me down at the vanity she took my hair out of braids and pulled part of it back. Leaving the short part of my frame falling softly down my cheek bone. She put on dark blue eye shadow going lighter then put on a light amount of mascara.

"Perfect she said stepping back. Now go change." Taking the clothes I changed into them and strapped on the chaps. Stepping out of the bathroom I realized Casey had my black hat in her hand and one of her own on her head. Putting on my hat Casey grabbed her bag and I put my phone and wallet in there with hers.

Locking our rooms we started our way down to the trailer the new bridle in my hand. The boys were already changed and tacking their horses up outside the trailer. Heading into the trailer I grabbed Winds lead rope and led him out, tying him to the bar next to Dante and Nick. Who both raised their heads at us when we came up,

"You ready for this?" I nodded. They'd told me the few patterns we would do during the parade and they were pretty simple. Stuff we do at school sometimes to warm up during practices.

Grabbing the western saddle I saddled Wind up and unbridled him just as the others started loading in their horses. Loading Wind up I kissed him on his nose and ducked out of the trailer and into the car. Wind had been acting really calm which confused me but I didn't question it and took it as a blessing.

"Alright let's get this show on the road," Adam said from the drivers seat as he pulls do it of the hotel parking lot and onto the street. Heading down the where they said the parade was starting. We had to park about a quarter mile away due to the cross but made it in time that we had a few floats left to go before us.

Wind was still acting strangely calm but I couldn't question it at the moment. Mounting up I smiled at the feel of the saddle.

"Y'all ready?" Casey asked from next to me at the front of the line, the line went Me, and Casey, Nick and Ben and Adam in the back. That way Wind didn't get frustrated with being behind the two geldings he didn't get along with well when riding and being next to Camelot seemed to calm him down. The person signaling everything signaled for us to go and we all picked up a fast walk. Smiling we all waved. We had on our SCRA Equestrian Jackets over our flannels advertising our flannels. As soon as the float in front of us slowed at a point I cued the first pattern which was basically cantering between each other, Nick, Adam and Ben going one way and me and Casey the other. Pulling out of the pattern I went in front of Casey and cued Wind to Canter forward a few steps then turn in tight and fast circles. He was basically spinning on his hind quarters and by the time we finished he and I were both panting.

Smiling at the crowds cheer I patted his neck,

"That's all for you boy, all for you," he snorted and we continued the parade but I didn't make him do the circle again. Adam and the others taking turns doing them.

"Thank you Stone Creek Riding Academy for Participating today! Leading their group today is SCRAs very own O'Connor Steele previously a barrel racer, now the team captain of the cross country team! With two of her teammates, Nick and Ben, and head of Show jumping Casey And O'Connor's brother Adam Steele," I rolled my eyes at the announcer of course they'd known about me previously barrel racing. Discounting Wind as we finished the parade I started to lead him to the trailer when I saw him limping. Stopping him. I clicked at him to pick up his front right hoof. He did reluctantly. It was warm. Really warm.

"ADAM!" My brother came jogging after handing Caesar's reins to Ben,

"What's wrong Connie?" I stepped out of the way,

"Feel , his front right hoof," his brows furrowed as he did. Stay her I'll have the others tie up their horses and we'll find someone who knows the vets number. Jogging with their horses to the trailer I stood with Wind murmuring to him reassuringly. I realized that we were one of the last ones to go and they were already picking up and it was dark. Shivering as a guest of wind blew as I heard a car swoosh by. Great. They opened the roads already. A large truck zoomed by honking its horn. Not good. Not good at all. Wind squealed and reared. Yanking the reins out of my hands going backwards. I heard people come up around me whispering and the flash of cameras. It only made Wind rear more. Looking at the crowd behind me I glared,

"Would you all shut up and stop taking pictures!" The whole crowd stopped moving and moved away from Wind giving him and me room. Where the heck were my friends! "Its alright Wind. It's alright" another person came up and took a picture. Flash on. Clearly thinking this was a show. Wind bolted. A car moving quickly down the road. A bush with a stick poking out of it off to the side. I made a split decision. Running into the road and in front of Wind I held the stick in my hand and lashed it at him. Pushing him back into the parking lot. He reared again but safe in the parking lot as the car zoomed by.

I looked at the stick in horror as Wind lashed out at me. Distrust in his eyes.

I just used a whip on my horse. On Wind.

I heard Adam Yell and I felt myself falling. Then everything went dark.

Chapter 13

"Here, let me help Connor," I shook my head at Adam as I slid out of our parents truck. My Knee in a brace. One week had passed. One week since Wind strained a tendon in his front right leg. One week since I woke up in a hospital my knee in a brace. One week since I've seen Wind. One week since I used a whip on Wind. Wind. The horse who's trust was broken so easily and won't let anyone near him.

Adam stood off to the side near by Casey next to me with my bag.

"Adam come help me with the horses," I heard my Dad call from by the trailer. I immediately started walking toward the house with a slight limp. You should be able to get back to riding a few weeks after school starts maybe even sooner my doctor said. A light fracture on your knee but it will heal much faster than a broken bone. Make sure you take it easy And keep your knee in the brace whenever your walking on it. The fracture though, where that came from. That came from Winds hoof coming down at me.

I blinked back the tears that were forming in my eyes and jogged up the stairs as fast as I could. Entering my room I heard Casey stay downstairs talking with my Mom. Collapsing on the bed sobs came out as I looked at the picture of me and Wind on my bed side table. I looked so happy. So carefree and Wind seemed to be nibbling on my hair and I was looking up at him in adoration.

"Why me? Why does this always happen to me?" I said as I heard my door open knowing it was my Mom,

"Oh sweetie," I felt her sit down beside me on my bed and start stroking my hair, "I don't know why bad thing happen to good people but I do know Fire isn't gone and Wind isn't gone either he just needs some help. Your both lost and he's waiting for you to find him."

I turned to look at her,

"But it's my fault we're lost in the first place," my Mom stayed silent for a moment before saying,

"You were trying save him not hurt him and I think he knows this. He just needs reassurance that you know this," I gave my Mom a hug,

"Thanks mom," sitting up I wiped away the tears that had started to run down my face. "I think I should probably go and save Casey from Dad and Adam," my Mom laughed,

"Now there's a good idea," hobbling down the stairs took some time but I made it. Making my way into the kitchen I found Adam and our Dad arguing about the best way to cook a burger and poor Casey sitting between them.

"Hey you two would you quit with the burgers. Poor Casey is our guest and here you are arguing with her in between you," my Mom said hands on her hips. My dad and brother immediately stopped arguing,

"Yes ma'am," I laughed as they said it in unison, Casey and Mom did as well.

"Now then it's Christmas eve tomorrow and we still need to bake cookies and you boys know the rules. No boys in the kitchen when the ladies are baking!" We all laughed as my Dad and Adam left the room to go watch Tv. Me and my Mom started grabbing ingredients while we instructed Casey on what to add and how much.

By the time we'd finished we had flour smeared all over our faces and clothes

Grinning I threw a towel at Casey,

"You've got a little something there," I said outlining her whole body. She laughed and I heard the door bell ring.

"I'll get it," hobbling to the door took longer than I thought but I made it.

"Hello-" I froze. Nick stood on the other side of the door, a bag by his feet.

"Nick? What're'ya doing here?" He smiled,

"Adam invited me to stay for a few days while my parents are out of town," I heard footsteps behind me,

"So your this Nick I've heard all about," I heard my Dad say,

"What type of riding you do? I I rolled my eyes,

"Why don't you come in first so my Dad can quiz you while your warm and not freezing. " he grinned and we moved out of the door way so he could come it,

"Nick! You made it! How was the trip?" I looked at Casey in shock so every one but me knew,

"It was good thanks," I whirled around to Adam,

"How come I'm the only one who didn't know Nick was coming?" Adam grinned sheepishly,

"Well you were kinda busy threatening every doctor in the hospital that if they didn't let you out soon you were gonna throw every horseshoe you could find at them," my jaw dropped,

"I didn't." He grinned even broader,

"You were kinda loopy on pain killers so yeah you did," I pinched the bridge of my nose and took a deep breath,

"If I find out your joking you Adam Mathew Steele are going to pay,"

"Good thing I'm not lying, now then Nicks not staying hallway so lets get him settled in the guest bedroom," I gave Adam a look,

"Casey's staying there, remember your girlfriend and my best friend," my parents were smart enough to sneak of away from the four crazy teenagers.

"Well then Casey can stay in your room," I sighed,

"Fine doofus of course she can,and I'm staying on the couch," they all gave me a look, and said at once,

"Like hell you are!" Adam spoke first,

"You have a fractured knee your not staying on the couch," I rolled my eyes,

"That's exactly why I am, it's a struggle to go up the stairs so it would make everyone's life easier if I slept on the couch and besides it's a pullout remember now go help Nick settle into the guest room and I'll help Casey," fuming Adam made his way up the stairs with Nick, weirdo and he wanted me and Casey to sleep in my room when we had a pullout couch. That was a kinda confusing argument I'll admit.

By the time Casey was settled in it was 7 o'clock and there were cookies waiting to be frosted downstairs.

Putting on Christmas music I started humming along as me and Casey started frosting the cookies and I looked at her a glint in my eye,

"Sooo Casey," Casey's head snapped up,

"Please tell me your not loopy on painkillers again I really don't want a horseshoe in my head," I laughed,

"No I was gonna ask what'd you get my brother?" I said grinning, they were so cute together after checking her gift I'd have to make sure my brother wasn't gonna mess up his,

"I got black leather halter with Caesars name engraved on it, I remember seeing yours on Wind and I noticed Adam didn't have one and I also got him a CD for Panic at the Disco's! Latest album with a signature from the lead singer!" Casey said excitedly. My jaw dropped. Well, that's the end of Adam how he's gonna top that, I have no idea.

"Okkk now I really wanna know what mine is," Casey grinned at my whining voice,

"Well you'll just have to wait till tomorrow," she sing songed. I started grumbling about the pains of waiting. Patience is a virtue. Horse poos a virtue.

. . .

By the time we finished the cookies and had watched a movie it was 11 and everyone was going up to bed. Me and Nick were the last ones up due to the fact Nick was still on the couch and I was sleeping on the couch so that boy needed to move so I could sleep!

"Well I guess I'll see you tomorrow, night Connor," I smiled at him,

"Night Nick, merry Christmas," when he finally made his way up the stair I sat for a few moment before I got up and limped to the doors pulling on my boots and jacket I made my way to the barn. I was crazy. I am definitely crazy. Entering the barn I welcomed the smell of horses and heard familiar whinnying. Fire. She was in the stall next to Wind and she recognized me immediately. Stroking her nose I smiled softly and moved onto Winds stall.

Going to Winds stall I looked at him my heart breaking a little. His coat was dirty due to no one Being able to clean it and his eyes held distrust in them. That was it. My mom was right. We were both lost and Wind was waiting for me to find him. Opening his stall I grabbed a lunging whip and used it to get Wind out of his stall and into the corral. In the corral I kept him moving which he did. I wanted my horse back and nothing was going to keep me from that.

I kept him going for what seemed like a few minutes but in reality it had been two hours. He still wouldn't gove. Damon his thoroughbred blood.

"I'm sorry Wind. I'm sorry! In was trying to help you! Not hurt you! I miss my best friend Wind! I want him back!" Winds bottom lip started sagging.

Flashback

"See here sweetie he's ready to join up,"

"How to you know granny?" She smiled at little 5 year old me,

"Its different for every horse they always give us a sign," she dropped the lunge whip and the horse immediately came over to her,

End of Flashback

I had learned everything I knew about join up from Granny and my Mom, they were the 'horse whisperers' in my family and they always said that I had both of their gifts combined. My Granny had past away about a year before my accident.

Taking a deep breath I dropped the lunging whip. This would either go terribly or wonderfully. Turning around I closed my eyes ready to give up after a moment when I heard hoof steps and a familiar nicker. I opened my eyes and turned around. Wind stood by me and nudged me with his nose. I threw my arms around his neck happy tears leaking out of my eyes as I whispered to him,

"I won't ever let you go Wind never again." Leading him back to his stall instead of going back inside I sat down in the corner of the stall and stayed with him as my eyes grew droopy with the need to sleep and slowly I fell into a peaceful sleep.

. . .

"Connor!!!"

"Ughhh do you have to yell!" I slowly lifted my head realizing I was in Winds stall as Casey came into the barn my family and Nick following.

"Geez no I don't have to yell when we wake up Christmas morning ready to open presents but no of course Connor decides to go missing so we spend the morning leaving the warm comfy house to find you in the barn in Winds. . . What'd I miss?" She stopped talking finally when she saw what horses stall I was in,

"We found each other again," my Mom smiled at me,

"Thats amazing honey, I always said you have more of a touch with horses than I ever did,"

"As your mother said that's great but it's cold and there's presents inside!" I laughed at my Dad as he motioned toward the house. Getting up we all made our way back to the house after feeding the horses quickly.

"Presents!" My brother yelled running into the living room we all followed but a little more slowly. All us ladies sat on the couch while the boys on the floor, of course, handed out presents,

"Umm this is Connors stack and this one Casey's" Adam said handing us two stacks and Nick my parents two stacks while they took their own on the floor.

I gasped as I opened the one from Casey as did Adam, she'd got me a necklace with two charms on it one of a horse with a flame in the middle of it and another with a gust of wind in the middle of it, symbolizing Wind and Fire.

I tackled Casey in a hug as did Adam and I laughed,

"Your not allowed to be this good at gifts!" Casey giggled in response and i pulled out of the hug and Adam kissed her forehead,

"Yes that is not allowed but I love them almost as much as you," I giggled at Casey's red face and realized I was the only one close enough to hear them. Yay I had blackmail! I scare myself sometimes.

"Casey stop spoiling our kids!" I kept on laughing and we continued opening presents. Mostly I got riding clothes, New headphones, and some gear for Wind. I also happily got a new phone case while was more simple but horse themed naturally. I now only had one present left as everyone else had just torn in there's. Picking it up I realized it was from Nick and slowly unwrapped it. Inside it was a beautiful engraved leather journal with a girl and horse free jumping on the cover.

"Thank you!" I basically tackled Nick as soon as I put it down.

"I'm glad you like it." I got off him and grinned,

"Well I mean who I wouldn't love a journal like that." He grinned back going back over to Casey, her and I spent the rest of the day beating the boys badly at Mario kart and telling stories with my parents. Overall not a bad day.

Looking out the window as it started growing dark I saw a few twinkling stars peek out and a full moon shine down. Next semester was going to be hard but I had a feeling no matter what my friends would be what got me through it. Especially Wind.

Chapter 14

Swinging my legs out of the car and hopping down I smiled as I took in the familiar sight of campus.

"Connor come help us with your horse!" I made my way to the back of the trailer where Caesar and Adam were walking down the rail. Hopping in on the side I spoke softly to Wind who was quite obviously not so happy at being trailered for so long,

"Easy boy your ok let's just get you out of the trailer huh? And then we can go for a nice long trail ride," the knee brace I had on reminded me just how much we'd gone through this past month. My knee was healed enough that we could ride...well in my opinion at least. Technically I wasn't allowed to ride for another month or so. Break had gone by quickly after Christmas and though I loved home I was happy to be back at SCRA.

I untied his lead rope and opened the bar when he stopped pawing his hoof. He hadn't been ridden since the beginning of break due to his strained ligament but he had just been cleared yesterday but I had been doing lots of ground work with him.

"Alright bud let's go," I clicked him on and his eyes flickered wildly. Not good. Not good at all. He tore off without anymore warning down the rail. Luckily unlike the last time he tore off at school he ran into the barn tearing through the aisles. Chasing after him as well as I could with my knee in its brace, I probably looked like a deranged person, I yelled as I went,

"Loose horse! Watch out!" When Wind finally stopped it was because a guy I didn't recognize was standing in front of him arms raised as Wind started rearing,

"Wind!" Winds ears perked at my voice and went back on all four legs. Going up besides him I took his lead rope and looked apologetically at the guy who'd stopped him, noticing his horse, a palomino with a white star, standing behind him.

"I am so sorry he hasn't done this in a long time,"

"Connor stop lying to the poor boy," I grinned when i heard one of my best friends voice,

"Meg!" We embraced and the poor guy stood there awkwardly as we laughed, turning back to him i smiled, "she's kinda right he does this a lot, thank you for stopping him otherwise I'd never have been able to catch him," he smiled and i realized he had blue eyes and dark brown almost black hair that was long on top and short on the sides. He was also seemed to be almost as tall as Nick,

"No problem, I'm Jeremy by the way Jeremy Johnson, this is actually kinda my first day," he said rubbing his horses neck, "and this is Venus,"

"I'm O'Connor Steele but call me Connor-" he cut me off,

"Wait didn't you used to barrel race?" I nodded slowly,

"Yeah but I don't barrel race anymore I event with this boy," I said patting Winds neck, "the crazy horse which you stopped is my boy Wind" he seemed a little shocked,

"Do you not recognize me?" I gave him a confused look,

"Well I would guess not, we only talked once, I was on the circuit with you, I did team roping, of course I'm here for cross country a kinda drastic change as well but yeah," Meg slapped her forehead,

"Oh I remember you, you rode the beautiful black stallion, I think his name was Bandit Heist," Jeremy nodded to her,

"Yep he's at my families farm, the wanted him to stay so they could breed him, pure quarter horse and quite headstrong as well," I smiled,

"I think I remember him I'm so sorry I didn't recognize you," I said a little embarrassed,

"You might know my brother Adam-"

"Who might know me?" I looked behind me to see Adam coming up with Caesar,

"Adam this is-"

"Jeremy Johnson I remember you from the circuit," Adam said cutting me off, again. They started rambling on about horses and everything else it seemed so I took the moment to sneak away with Wind and put him in his stall, Meg right behind me.

"So wanna get your stuff in your food then ride the horses to the cafe?" I nodded.

Making our way out i saw my parents had unloaded our stuff and were waiting to head out. Giving them each a hug goodbye my mom whispered in my ear,

"You remember just how much you and Wind have been through and you keep it close to your heart," nodding my head I clutched my Mom tighter for a moment before releasing her. Smiling softly she waved as she and my Dad got back into the truck.

"I take it our Dream team is back to normal?" I nodded and we headed to the dorms to change for a ride.

As I pulled on breeches, my paddock boots and half chaps. I was just putting my knee brace back on when Casey walked in, a wild grin on her face. Oh boy.

"So...did you meet Jeremy?" I nodded slowly, "did you know he's our new teammate and dormie?" I really was dense sometimes. He said he did cross country and he was new it makes sense he would be taking Wills place. Taking my silence as an answer Casey grinned even more,

"He's also quite cute you know..." Rolling my eyes I walked out of the room waving at her behind me. Yeah sure having a boyfriend might be nice but I was sixteen and had some time before just figured that out. I mean I was still figuring out myself and wind. Besides Jeremy probably will get asked out within the week... he was rather good looking.

Annnd my butt was on the floor again rubbing my forehead I groaned,

"How many times are we going to do this Nick," a tanned hand with a black ring on the middle finger appeared in front of me,

"Sorry, I'm not Nick though if that helps," my cheeks turned cherry.

"Sorry Jeremy didn't mean to go off on you there. I guess I should be the one apologizing as this isn't the first time it's happened." I said taking his hand and he pulled me up.

"No problem guessing know now to look out for girls falling on their butts," I rolled my eyes and let go of his hand as I stood on my own. He was now grinning and what do I see? Dimples. The dang dude had dimples. Curse you world for good looking guys!

"Well anyways I've gotta get going Megs waiting for me at the barn." He smiled again,

"I was actually headed there to go on a trail ride and I then realised I don't know any of the trails..." I grinned this time,

"We're heading to a cafe that's at the end of a trail on campus if you want to come?" He nodded and we made our way out of the dorm and to the barn. Meg was waiting by Winds stall Calypso by her side with only a bridle on.

"I thought you were never gonna get here!" I grinned,

"Yeah yeah I know. Meg you met Jeremy earlier I invited him to come along with us," she nodded and I headed to the tack room Jeremy in tow to get Winds bridle while he got Venus'. I had checked with him on the way over that he could ride bareback. Cuz that's the way we roll. Snagging his bridle I made my way back to Winds stall and slipped it over his head as he looked out to see me coming.

Opening his stall I started to vault onto his back. And my butt ended on the floor again.

"You ok?" Meg asked her eyebrow raised in surprise. I hadn't missed a vault onto a horse since we first learned.

I nodded and a hand appeared in front of me again.

"I think your becoming to friendly with falling on your butt," I chuckled at Jeremy and let him pull me up,

"Yeah I kind forgot that I wouldn't be able to vault up with my knee in a brace,"

"How about I give you a leg up today then?" I shrugged and he laced his fingers together putting my uninjured knee in it he pushed me up till I was sitting comfortably on Winds back. Jeremy then pulled himself up onto Venus which wasn't much of a feat considering he was tall and Venus was only about 15 hh.

"Now then, shall we get this show on the road?" Grinning Meg nudged Calypso into a canter towards the trail. Nudged Wind lightly he followed, Jeremy and Venus not far behind.

"Log ahead!" Crap. I gripped my knee with one hand. It's fine. I'd make it. Calypso made it over and prepared Wind to Jump. Wind took most of my weight as I clutched to his back my knee not able to grip him. But we made it. Slowing to a trot by Meg I massaged my knee lightly. Meg didn't know that I wasn't supposed to ride but what she didn't know wouldn't hurt her. Turning behind me I saw Venus and Jeremy jump with inches to spare which was impressive considering it was a rather large log.

Coming to a walk besides me he grinned,

"I can't wait to get back onto a real cross country course. Any clue what the cross country teams like here?" I connected dots again. I was an idiot. He was joining the team I was team captain of.

"Well, um, you see-"

"Connors cross country captain!" I rolled my eyes as Meg cut me off. Why I was trouble getting that out I have no idea but leave it to Meg to fill in the gaps. Jeremy grinned,

"You didn't tell me why?" I smiled sheepishly,

"Yeah it kind took me a bit to connect the dots. Sorry I'm sometimes really slow when it's not about horses," He laughed,

"Don't worry I can relate," I grinned in response.

"Well if you two are done shall we?" Meg said laughing a bit. I looked up to see another log coming up and grinned at Jeremy and Meg,

"Last one there buys!" I called back to them as Wind and I took off momentarily forgetting my knee. Not a good idea. We took the log at a usual cross country speed and I started to slip only gripping Winds Mane in order to keep myself on. Seeming to feel my discomfort Wind slowed almost immediately after we jumped and let me right myself.

How I loved this horse.

Nudging him back into a canter we left the others behind again easily out pacing them with Winds wide stride. Smiling I applied a bit of pressure to the reins and he slowed almost immediately. Ever since the accident he seemed much more sensitive to his rider. At least me.

"So any clue who is taking Sonias' place?" Meg asked me as she caught up and we slowed our horses to a walk, Jeremy coming up on my other side.

"Not a clue hopefully someone who can ride though," Meg nodded,

"Who else is on the team?" Jeremy asked from my other side,

"Well let's see, there's Nick and his grey gelding Dante. Ben and his horse Star, they've got a pretty good bond and he's you roommate, heh should've said that first," I said rubbing the back of my neck "then there's Ally and Lukas I hate to say it but I haven't gotten to know them quite well but I do know that they're good riders. And there's me, the team captain that fractured her knee the day before break and has a blooded thoroughbred," I finished grinning. He whistled,

"Sounds like quite a team," I nodded and I heard a sputter on my other side,

"You're riding with a fractured knee!" Oops, Meg started rambling about how stupid I am and I probably didn't help when I said I technically wasn't supposed to put to much pressure on my knee. Meg shook her head when she finished her rant,

"What am I going to do with you O'Connor Steele?"

Chapter 15

Sliding into a booth a laughed as Jeremy told us about how his old horse Bandit once completely tossed him onto the ground when a little five year-old girl approached him with a balloon and lollipop.

"It was terrible her mom must've reprimanded me for almost twenty minutes...it was terrifying!" I giggled,

"Sounds like it..." I said trailing off as my phone buzzed. My Mom's number came up, "hey guys give me a second my mom's calling me," they nodded and continued talking as. I slid out of the booth and went outside,

"Hey Mom what's up?"

"Hey sweetie so I have a question to ask you,"

"Yeah shoot,"

"So do you remember our family friend Anna?" I nodded then remembered she couldn't see,

"Yeah she's my age and rides as well right?" I heard a shuffle, she totally just nodded, I chuckled under my breath as she realized what she did, like mother like daughter I guess,

"Well, the horse she leased, Shadow was just put down," I gasped I remembered that horse, he was a big warmblood almost all brown but had wisps of black covering him like a blanket, and he was such a sweetie.

"That's terrible! What happened?" Her mom sighed,

"I think it was a freak accident," man, I know how it feels,

"That's even worse,"

"Yes and that's where you come it...Anna is an amazing jumper, she hasn't been riding that long but she's amazing, been placing at all the shows. Anyways my point sorry, there's an open spot at SCRA," I saw where this was going,

"She managed to convince her parents to let her go, next year...but she needs a horse and I know an exceptional little jumper that's sitting in our barn right now," she was talking about Flame. While yes she was Fire's daughter she was 3/4 Arabian and an amazing jumper. Standing at 14.9 hands high she wasn't exactly large and she looked more Arabian that her half quarter horse Mom. She was also only 5 1/2 so still a work in progress.

"Mom, I'd need to see Anna ride her first. You think you can set up a time for her to come ride Flame and then maybe. Just face time me during their ride and I'll decide then," I said, that seemed reasonable, Flame was important to me so i needed to know who I was handing her over to.

"That sounds great! I'll let you know then!" I smiled, I loved flame and Flame loved to jump but I had wind and she needed a rider so this is a good idea.

"Alright bye Mom, love you,"

"Love you too sweetie I'll talk to you later," hanging up I slipped my phone into my back pocket and went back into the cafe.

Sliding into the booth Meg looked at me,

"So what'd your Mom want?"

"Oh something about one of our horses Flame, did you guys order yet?" Jeremy nodded,

"Meg ordered you a burger, fries and Oreo milkshake," I grinned,

"You know me to well Meg, too well," she grinned,

"Yes I do, yes I do," laughing we continued talking as our food was served and my phone vibrated again as we started finishing up,

Nick: hey, where you at??

Connor: At the Cafe with Meg and the new kid Jeremy, why?

Nick: Just curious

Connor: Alrighty, wanna go for a ride when I get back Wind looks bored, looking out the window which was by where the horses were tied up I snapped a picture of him and sent it to Nick

Nick: definitely, who can resist that face lol

Connor: cool see you then :)

Smiling I started to look up and my phone was snatched. Oh boy.

"So who we smiling so goofy at Huh Connor?" I shook my head at Meg. "Oh Nick, didn't he stay with you over break?"

"Yes Meg, he did," Jeremy raised an eyebrow at me,

"You two dating?" I shook my head quickly, my face turning red as I hid it in my hands,

"Oh they should be" Meg said grinning, "I call them Connick!" Jeremy laughed and they started chanting as I groaned...loudly.

"Well if your done reading my texts I've gotta go I told Nick I'd go on a ride. A chorus of 'oohs' came from them. "I'll see you two later," they laughed at my embarrassed state and I took my phone back from Meg, putting it on silent.

Leading wind to the steps I was able to use the tallest step to hop on his back and head toward the barn. Taking the shorter way-that didn't have jumps- I pushed Wind into a slow canter and we quickly made it to the barn where Nick was waiting with Dante in Jeans, a SCRA green hoodie and boots.

"Hey," he said as I stopped Wind in front of hmm,

"Hey, you ready to go?" He nodded and pulled himself onto Dante who I realised also wasn't wearing a saddle.

"I take it no jumping trails?" Nick said and I nodded. He knew all to well I wasn't supposed to be riding, especially jumping. "I know the perfect trail then, come on," I nodded and I pulled Wind up next to Dante as we rode side by side onto the trail. We didn't really talk but we occasionally looked at each other. Reaching to my neck I played with the necklace he'd given me for Christmas. I hadn't taken it off since.

"So, a family friend of mine is going to come here next year," Nick looked at me,

"That's cool what style does she ride?"

"She's a show jumper but the horse she leased was recently put down so my Mom asked me if I'd be ok with her riding Flame." His eyes widened,

"What'd you say?"

"I told her that she needed to face time me to watch their ride one time so I could see how they worked. And besides Flames only 5 1/2 and she's spirited. I want to make sure the rider is soft but can put her foot down when need be." He nodded,

"That makes sense. Let me know when your going to watch her ride and I'll watch with if you want," I though for a moment,

"Yeah that'd actually be great," he smiled,

"Cool" and yet again we fell in a comfortable silence. The sun was starting to set and I was about to say we should turn back when Nick pointed to something up ahead,

"Look," there was a beautiful pond up ahead with fireflies lingering in the air. I gasped, the water sparkled with the remaining sunlight.

"Lets go closer!" I said grinning, Nick grinned back and dismounted. As I dismounted I felt my knee give and as I started falling warm hands were on my waist keeping my upright. Looking up green eyes stared back I don't know how long we stayed like that, we just stood there until I pulled back a bit turning around.

Looking up again Nicks eyes were flickering and I wrapped my arms around his midsection my head leaning on his chest and he leaned his cheek on my head arms still wrapped around my waist.

"Connor," I looked back up at him, he was about to say something else, but he seemed to change his mind as the next thing I know his lips were on mine. My eyes widened but I quickly melted into the kiss moving my arms so they wrapped around his neck on hand buried in his hair as one of his hands moved up my back to cup the base of my neck.

Eventually we both pulled back smiling slightly. Moving one of my arms I started to play with one of his hoodie strings my forehead leaning on his,

"You have no idea how long I've wanted to do that," he mumbled. I grinned,

"True," looking up I looked him in the eyes and asked the most cliche question ever,

"What's this make us?" He smiled,

"If your up for it, O'Connor Steele, will you be my girlfriend?" I grinned again,

"Nick , it would be my honor," he grinned in return and kissed me again spinning me around as we came out of it. Laughing he set me back on my own two feet,

"I think we should head back, it's almost dark," I said against his chest, "Leg up?" He stepped back as we walked over to where the horses had wandered to. It seemed Dante and Wind were finally getting along. I grabbed Winds reins and waited for Nick to come over with Dante to Leg me up. Hands wrapped around my hips and i was suddenly sitting on Wind.

Looking down I saw Nick grinning at me,

"Thought that'd be easier," I rolled my eyes and turned Wind as he mounted up,

"Wanna canter?" He asked bringing Dante next to wind, I smiled,

"Lets go," nudging Wind and kissing at him I was soon in his rocking canter, Dante and Nick right next to us. The barn was soon in sight. Nudging Nick into a gallop as we came into the grass I let out a loud laugh as the wind blew in my hair. I heard a shout as Nick got Dante to gallop trying to catch us. As we came to the doors I slowed Wind and threw up my arms,

"I win!" I cheered laughing as Dante and Nick came to a stop a moment later. Nick hopped off Dante rolling his eyes,

"No you cheated!" I snickered,

"That what losers say!" I said in a sing song voice as I started to dismount. Yet again warm hand were on my waist supporting me as I hopped down. Grinning up at Nick I pressed a kiss upside down on his pouting lips and used the moment to sneak out of his grasp and lead Wind into the barn. Nick grumbling behind my with Dante. We led our horses into their stalls and gave them a good quick curry. Stepping out of Winds stall I made my way to my tack locker and quickly put away my bridle.

Peeking around the corner I saw Nick rubbing Dantes' head outside of his stall, a content smile on his face. Sneaking up on him I wrapped my arms around his midsection burying my face in his back. Taking a deep breath I realized he smelled like Pine soap. Smiling softly as Nick turned around, he wrapped me up in a hug as well as I closed my eyes against his chest shivering slightly at the cool night air that blew through the barns open doors.

Stepping back Nick pulled his hoodie over his head and pulled it over my own. Grinning I slid my arms into the sleeves and burrowed into its warmth and leaned back against him as he wrapped his arms around me again,

"You know your brother is going to kill me right?" I looked up at him and laughed at his serious face,

"He'll probably give you a really dumb talk and then slap you on the back. Actually after he finds out he'll probably sit in a desk chair and pet a fake cat and say, 'so you want to date my baby sister' and he and Casey will plan to interrogate us at the same time" Nick let out a loud laugh, "Megs Been shipping us so beware tonight," Nick kept laughing,

"I can totally see that!" I laughed along with him,

"We should probably head back though. School starts tomorrow," he nodded and with one arm around my shoulders with me burrowed into his side, we walked back to the dorm.

Entering the dorm a light clicked on. Oh boy, here we go.

"I told you so!!!" I looked over to see Ben and Meg jumping up from the couch and Meg pointing at me. Ben to, so she told Ben about her ship as well!

"Ok fine you were right, your were right," Meg did some sort of silly jig and then turned serious,

"How long? Please tell me only tonight! Jeremy and I have a bet! Well Ben also bet, but he and Jeremy teamed up so anyways...how long!!" I grinned, while Nick stood awkwardly next to me his arm still on my shoulders.

"Ben you and Jeremy owe Meg some money," Meg did her silly Jig again while Ben groaned and fell back onto the couch. Meg fell back next to him giggling and kicking her socked feet in the air.

Taking the moment to sneak away me and Nick snuck up the stairs and I giggled softly at Nicks exasperated expression. Stopping at my door Nick wrapped me in a hug again and I pecked him on the lips.

"Thank you," I said as I stepped away hand on the door knob,

"I'll see you tomorrow," he said grinning as he turned and made his was to his room. As I entered Casey and Is' room. A light clicked on in our room and I heard a shout from upstairs. Totally called it. Casey turned in the desk chair stroking a stuffed cat.

"I've been waiting for you Connor... we need to talk," I broke down laughing. I know them both way to well.

"Yes I'm dating Nick now. We kissed tonight and we are boyfriend and girlfriend. No we didn't wait to tell you, We just got back," Casey started laughing,

"I've been wanting to do that for so long!" I grinned,

"I know Casey, I know," laughing I sat on my bed and she faced me in the chair, the cat still in her lap,

"So how are you with it?" I smiled softly,

"Really good Casey, really happy," she smiled,

"That's great Connor,"

It is. It really is.

Chapter 16

"Alright guys, I know your curious why I called you here," all the advanced show jumping, advanced Dressage and naturally advanced cross country teams were all assembled in arena one and all of our instructors stood at the front as they took turns talking, Josie starting it off,

"As you all know we have qualified for finals. Now finals is very different from anything you've ever done. As you know when you tried out for your teams we tested you in each discipline. This is where it get complicated. Each team will be split up with two of one discipline in each group." Immediately murmuring started. Josie was right this was going to be very different, another instructor stepped forward i figured she was the dressage instructor from her instructor jacket,

"No team will be allowed to have two team captains on it as the team captains will work together to create their teams. And last but not least the competition will be held next year on March twentieth. While yes we are qualified there are many more competitions to come before we are ready. Now then, seniors and those who cannot return next year please stand." At least four seniors stood including Lukas and Ally from my cross country team and one from the other teams as well as two others who wouldn't be returning stood.

I gasped, Amy who was on the dressage team and in my dorm was standing. I hadn't gotten to know her very well but I knew she was wonderful at dressage and a nice person and someone on the show jumping team was standing as well. This wasn't good each team was going to need at least two more members. We were still missing one since Sonia left, luckily Jeremy had taken Wills' place not to mention Jeremy was actually a freshman but the other dorms were full so they just tossed him in with our sophomore dorm since we had an open bed though he'd be with sophomores again next year when we moved dorms.

"I know this doesn't look good but we already have prospects to take their places," the instructor continued,

"I assume I should've introduced myself to those who don't know me, I am Callia Larson the advanced Dressage instructor. You will all become very familiar with me very soon." She nodded her head to us all and stepped back then the man that was standing by Josie stepped forward,

"I am Lewis Hamilton the show jumping instructor and I already know most of you but for those who don't know me I tell you this, focus on what you want and you'll reach amazing heights and I hope to help both you and your horse get there," I grinned he wasn't my show jumping instructor because he specialized with the advanced show jumping team, but I could already tell I'd enjoy working with him.

"I know this is a lot of information to take in and for those leaving us we will all miss s you and we hope to see you in the future." He continued and I saw a few of the seniors with saddened faces, "one more thing, as for the prospects we have been looking at We'd like captains to join us on a trip in 1 month to help with evaluating them," my eyes widened as I remembered Anna was one of them. I started to squirm I needed to see her on Flame and soon.

"Now then we expect you all to be practicing and preparing for the selections. Captains start thinking about this all. We know these teams will go far. You are all dismissed," I looked at Nick whose brows were furrowed, thinking.

"Next year is going to be nuts," he nodded. It was currently March 17th and we'd officially been together for about a month and a half. I still hadn't been completely cleared by the doctor so I still had to wear a knee brace but I could ride, well with the doctors consent this time. School was out in two months and two weeks but it was going to be a whirlwind till then.

Standing I reached my hand to him and he looked up before intertwining his fingers with mine and stood up. Casey came up on my other side with Adam. While Adam wasn't technically on these advanced teams he'd started interning with the vet on campus and was now going on all the trips with the team's for experience and just in case of any sudden emergencies. Casey on the other hand was on advanced show jumping naturally although she wasn't captain.

"You guys think we'll make it?" I asked them,

"Of course, it'll take a lot of work but otherwise we'll be fine." Casey said her voice not holding a sliver of doubt.

"I think your right...and did you know Amy was leaving?" I asked Casey,

"Yeah there was something going on at home so she decided to leave. Megan's getting a new roommate next year though," I looked around and saw Meg talking to Amy now there was a lot of hugging and talking. Ben stood by Megs side, his hands in his pockets. They weren't a couple yet but they'd gotten really close recently. I looked at my own boyfriend,

"I need to see Anna on flame and soon," he nodded in agreement,

"We can call your mom when we're back at the dorm and set it up," I smiled and leaned into him as he put his arm around my shoulder and kissed my forehead. I heard gagging,

"No PDA in front of the older brother please!" I laughed at Adams antics and Casey as she slapped his arm in retaliation,

"She can say the same thing about PDA in front of little sisters you know!" He placed an obnoxious kiss on her lips silencing her and I gagged this time,

"No PDA!" We all started to laugh as Casey started to tell Adam off.

...

"Hey sweetie! What's up?" My Mom said cheerfully her hair it's usual braid. I grinned, Nick and I were sitting on my bed and I'd just face timed my Mom. We had headed to my room to call her right after the meeting had ended,

"Hey Mom, so I was just told that as a captain I'm going to be evaluating new prospects for the team's. Including Anna," Mom nodded,

"Your spring breaks in two weeks right?" Mom asked and I nodded, "why don't we have you come watch her and flame then," I grinned,

"Mom that's perfect! I'll actually be able to see them work together in person. Can't believe I didn't think of that!" I heard a chuckle next to me and I elbowed Nick in the stomach.

"Alright honey, I'll call Anna's Mom right now and set it up.," Mom said, "I'll talk to you later sweetie, Love you!"

"Love you too Mom, bye" I said hanging up. I leaned back against Nick who wrapped his arm around me.

"You think they'll be good together?" He asked,

"I hope so," I mumbled into his chest. Pulling myself out of his grip I kicked off my boots and pulled on his sweatshirt that was handing on my bed post. Snuggling back into his side I closed my eyes as he wrapped his arms around me yet again.

"You just gonna take a nap there?" He said chuckling, his chest vibrating against my cheek as I nodded. "Alright then, I'll wake you up when it's time for practice," I nodded again already drifting off as he placed a soft kiss on my head.

I had drifted off for no more than 10 minutes when my door swung open slamming as it did waking me immediately.

"CONNOR!!!!" Oh boy, I lifted my head from Nicks chest as Ben stormed in Megan right behind him,

"What do you want now?" Nick said his voice crabby,

"We need her to settle something! Who's horse is faster Calypso or Star?" I laughed,

"Calypso's a dressage horse, Stars a cross country horse, obviously Star is and even if Star wasn't Star would outlast Calypso easily," I said calmly, "now out!!!! I need a nap!!" I yelled throwing a pillow at them, they ducked and ran out Ben calling out as they did,

"Oooh Nicks gonna get someeeee," a I groaned as I heard footsteps barrel up the stairs and my brother burst into the room. No way I was getting a nap now, sitting up fully Nick and I climbed down my loft beds ladder as Adam berated us.

"Nick five feet from my baby sis at all times!" I rolled my eyes and grabbed a pair of navy breeches, my paddock boots and half chaps slipping out of the room leaving my boyfriend subject to my brothers berating g. Moving quickly down the hallway I slipped into Megan's room.

"I knew it!!" I yelled catching Meg and Ben mid make out on Megs bed. Ben's head snapped up and he jumped up enough that he fell off Megs bed and onto the floor groaning. While Meg sat red faced on her bed, "I knew something was going on but I waited so you could tell me well the jig is up missy! You didn't tell me so I caught you red handed!" By the end of my rant I was panting, "Now then I am borrowing your bathroom to change because my brother is berating my boyfriend because of yours!" Turning heel I walked into Meg and Amy's bathroom closing the door behind me.

I grinned to myself as I changed into my breeches and boots leaving Nicks sweatshirt on I headed out of the bathroom and saw the two lovebirds had left. marching back to my room I dropped my jeans off, seeing it was clear of a yelling brother and scared boyfriend. Heading downstairs I saw the dorm was gathered at the kitchen island. Casey seemed to be yelling at Megan for not telling her about Ben and her. Using the yelling as a distraction I slipped out the front door about to head to the barn when two arms circled around my waist picking my up.

"You left me for dead you know," I laughed as Nick threw me over his shoulder marching to the barn I guessed as I heard familiar nickers a few moments later.

"You can put me down now, Nick," I said my voice sounding funky from my upside down Position,

"Nah I think I'm good," I groaned and pounded my first into his back,

"Put. Me. Down!" Nick laughed and did as I said catching me as I wobbled. "See that wasn't so hard," I said hands on my hips as I turned around refusing to look at him, nose in the air,

"Yes, Connor, yes it was," Nick said stepping closer his hot breath sending a shiver down my back as he leaned down closer to me. Turning me around Nick grinned at my breathless face and pulled me in for a kiss. Acting on instinct I wrapped my arms around his neck pulling him closer and deepening the kiss. His hand trailed down my back stopping at my waist his other hand cupping my head. Pulling apart I leaned my forehead against his breathing in his woodsy smell.

"I'm happy Nick, for the first time in a long time I'm really happy." I said, Nick smiled pecking my lips before answering,

"Me too Connor, me too," he mumbled against my own lips. Grinning I snuck out of his arms and into Winds stall hugging his head to my chest.

"Hey boy. You want to go for a ride?" I whispered into his ear,

"Hey, so now that your done saying hello to your other boy mind giving me a few tips on my barrel racing again?" I turned around grinning at my boyfriend.

"Well I mean as long as Wind doesn't mind," Nick pouted and I laughed,

"I guess it'd be alright. I'll take Wind with I wouldn't mind running around the barrels again," Nick gave me surprised look. I'd told him most of my past just not all of it. Only a handful of people knew my whole past. Will was one I realised with a frown but quickly shook my head clear of my thoughts and slid on Winds Halter leading him to the cross ties before grabbing my familiar western saddle and bridle. Grooming Wind next to Dante and Nick I hefted the saddle up on Winds back. My hands running over the familiar patterns memories flashing at the back of my mind. Tightening his girth I turned to Nick a sad smile playing on my lips,

"You ready to go?" He nodded taking Dantes reins following me to the arena. Mounting easily in the western saddle I settled into the familiar grooves and led Wind off to the side as Nick made his was to the gate way. Nodding to Nick he took of kicking Dante into a canter as they sped around the barrels. Memories kicked into my mind as I watched them run.

"They're unstoppable folks nothing can stop them now!"

"Nothing but a blur of fire!"

Silent tears trickled down my face. But instead of a frown overtaking my face a small smile slipped onto it. These were happy tears now. Fire was alive and safe and I was ok. I looked up and saw Nick come up beside me breathing a little heavier from the run. Adrenaline no doubt still pumping in his veins.

"You ok?" I nodded smiling and leaned overspending a quick kiss on his lips.

"Its time you saw just exactly who I was." I said turning Wind to the categorizing Nick sitting on Dante a confused look of his face.

Going into the gate I leaned low over Winds neck and kicked him on. His gallop taking the arena by storm. The wind. The rush. All of it blew away the tears that had been sitting in my heart and mind for too long.

Chapter 17

"Connorrrrrrr" I rolled over onto my side to see Adam standing on my ladder,

"Why are you waking me up. So. Early. On. The. Weekend?" I grumbled sitting up,

"Mom and Dad are going to be here in half an hour so I figured I should tell you to get packed seeing as you haven't yet." I shoved him off the ladder. He somehow landed on both feet as I climbed down.

Of course he was right, I hadn't packed yet. Getting dressed quickly in jeans, a tee shirt and Nicks hoodie I quickly threw riding clothes into my duffel with my half chaps as well. Everything else I needed was already at our house as I didn't take all my clothes with me and my bathroom stuff I had packed the night before.

Zipping my duffel I quickly braided my hair and pulled on my hat before lugging my bag downstairs. Adam and I were one of the last two to leave as everyone else had left the day before.

"Adam? Where you at!" I called in the silent dorm. No one answered. Shrugging I went out the front door, he was probably getting the horses set to go. Jogging over to the barn I saw a familiar trailer and truck parked in front of it. Breaking into a run I dropped my duffel besides it and launched myself onto the back of my Mom who stood watching my Dad and brother.

"Mom!" My Mom turned and gave me a large bear hug,

"Oh Connor sweetie I missed you!" I felt another pair of arms encircle us,

"Hey baby girl," I smiled even more and hugged my Dad as well. Pulling away I saw my Dad frown when he saw the sweatshirt I was wearing.

"Connor...who's sweatshirt is that," I looked at my Mom. She said she would tell him about Nick and I since he was even more overprotective than Adam. My Mom shrugged. Gee thanks Mom. I looked back at my Dad,

"ItsNicks" I spit out quickly before running over to Wind who was currently prancing around in his stall as Adam led Caesar by and not giving my Dad a chance to reply. Pressing a kiss to Winds muzzle I ran into the tack room and pulled out all his shipping things. Jogging back to Wind I slipped on his halter and strapped on his shipping boots before leading him out to the trailer. Seeing he was locked in I exited the trailer and nodded to Adam who swung up the ramp and locked the door. Jogging back into the barn I led my mom to my tack locker and grabbed Winds all purpose saddle, his usual bridle, western saddle, and polos. Giving my mom the western saddle I took the rest as we headed back to the trailer and loaded it into the storage compartment in the trailer. Smiling at my mom we swung my duffel in as well and got into the truck with the boys.

And we were off.

...

"Connor, we're here," my eyes shot open as we pulled up to our familiar house and barn. Grinning I jumped out of the car as it pulled to a stop and ran to the trailer swinging open the door and dropping the ramp I jogged up it to my favorite boy. I dropped a kiss on his cheek before leading him out of the trailer a happy skip in my step at being home. Entering the barn I smiled as I was met with friendly knickers and a warm smell of hay and horses. Taking off Winds' boots I set him loose into his stall and said hello to my two baby girls. Stroking both Flame and Fires muzzles at the same time I placed a kiss on each horses head and looked at Flame.

"Hey baby girl, you're gonna get a rider soon hopefully. Can you promise to be good?" I whispered to her, Flame snorted as if to say,

'We'll we'd with one last kiss on both my girls and my boy I headed back out to help unload the tack. While I loved SCRA, I loved home just as much.

Two days later

"Yeah she's coming today," I replied to Nick through the phone as I set it on speaker so I could braid my hair. We had taken to calling each other every morning and night plus I had promised to facetime him while Anna rode Flame today.

"Try to go easy on her Connor," he said through the phone a slight chuckle in his laugh. I rolled my eyes,

"When do I ever not go easy?" I could literally hear him raising his eyebrow, "but yes I will try to go easy on her,"

"That's good enough for me. I've got to go meeting up with some old friends from the stable so just text me when it's time. Love you," I grinned,

"Love you too Nick, talk to you later," with that I hung up and pulled on my equestrian hat before heading downstairs clothed in navy riding pants, a black tank top, and my hat with my boots plus half chaps in hand.

"Connor!" I walked into the kitchen just as my Mom called my name,

"That's my name!" I answered happily, my Mom smacked me with a towel and handed me alfalfa a bagel with cream cheese.

"Walk and eat Anna's arriving any moment now and you need to get Flame," I nodded and stuck my bagel in my mouth while I pulled on my boots. Ready to go I jogged out to the barn greeting each horse minus Flame who was in the paddock.

Sending out a whistle as I arrived at the paddock halter and lead rope in hand Flame cantered over to me ears perked. She skidded to a stop and thrust her nose into my pockets.

"No treats for you greedy," I said laughing.

"Now let's get going," slipping on the halter I led her into the barn and tacked her up managing to finish just as a silver Toyota highlander pulled up. I held up my hand in greeting as two people exited the car. Anna and who I'm guessing is her sister based on the fact they looked similar and her sister while older not nearly old enough to be her mom.

"Long time not see Anna," I said with a grin. She was around my height with Dark Auburn hair and light green eyes that looked like they held some sort of secret and almost daring anyone who looked to try and find that secrecy. I really did make weird observations about people...

"Sorry if I don't remember you well," she said with a small sheepish smile. I waved my hand,

"Eh it's fine, I mean I may or may not have forgotten about you until my Mom reminded me," Anna laughed,

"Now as fun talking to me may be we have a horse for you to ride!" I said happily leading her to the barn. Looking at her out fit I realised she was dressed for whatever. Jeans, paddock boots, half chaps, a t-shirt and a helmet in her hand but a black ball cap on her head while her hair was pulled back in a knot. I liked her even more already.

"Now then the lady of the our...Dancing in the Flames!" I said happily revealing Flame who stood in the cross ties. Anna approached her slowly offering her hand for Flame to sniff. Flame rubbed her nose on the palm of her hand and immediately went to sniffing her pockets. I nearly slapped head. That mare loved her treats way to much. Luckily Anna just laughed and pulled a treat out of her pocket and after getting nod from me fed it to the little mare.

"Now then how about we see you go around on her," I said with a grin. Anna nodded and handed her hat to her sister and buckled her helmet before taking Flames reins. Showing her to the paddock I have her a leg up and jogged to the fence pulling up face time on my phone.

"My boyfriend wants to see you ride if that's all right he's pretty good at judging a rider and horse together," I said as Anna circled Flame around the arena a quick walk to warm her up. A curt nod had me dialing Nick.

"Hey, she here?" I nodded and heard noise in the background but couldn't see why a yell told me why,

"Hey Nick hope your girlfriend knows the mess she's gotten herself into!" I heard laughter as Nick yelled back at his friends,

"Oh bug off Jason!" Chuckling I flipped the camera around onto Anna and Flame who were now trotting smoothly around the arena. I had set up a few cross rails for them night before and figured it was now or never.

"Alright Anna taker over the cross rails!" I called over to her. I saw a small smile sneak onto her face before she had Flame in a canter headed towards the cross rails. My jaw nearly dropped as they went over them. They were perfect. Even when Flame let out a buck in between them Anna had ridden smoothly and got Flame over safely. This girl was going to be a great addition to SCRA. I flipped the camera back around and saw Nick had the same expression almost as I did.

"They almost looked like you and Wind just softer," I nodded and turned to her sister who had stood by quietly a proud smile on her face,

"I think they're a perfect match," the sisters smile grew,

"You have no idea how happy this will make her," I nodded,

"I think...I think I do," grinning I waved Anna over.

"So Anna," I started as she stopped Flame in front of me, "I hear you're gonna be pretty big competition at SCRA," Anna's smile grew as she realised what I was saying.

"You missy, just got yourself a horse for the academy," Anna looked like she was holding back a shout,

" thank you, thank you, thank you! I promise we won't let you down!" I laughed as Anna hopped off flame and gave me a big hug before hugging Flame and placing a big kiss on her muzzle.

"So I have to go back to school next week but you are welcome to come and ride her when you can. You can even set up certain times with my Mom," I said as Anna stroked Flames neck and nodded,

"Sounds good, although I have a job at the stable I used to ride at so I can't come out here more than three times a week," I nodded,

"Thats fine, besides the summer is coming up and when I'm back I can help you and Flame get ready. Although I do need to warn you, team captains and trainers and going to be scouting on all the new advanced team members so be prepared," Anna nodded,

"Don't worry, we will be," I grinned I was liking this girl more and more.

"Connor! Can I say hi now?" I let out a laugh and looked down at my phone realising Nick was still there,

"Sorry," holding up my phone I introduced them through the screen, "Nick this Anna as you know and Anna this is my boyfriend Nick, he wanted to see you ride as he's better at stadium show jumping then i am even though he's on the cross country team," Anna smiled shyly,

"Nice to meet you,"

"Nice to meet you too, now I gotta run my friends are about to attack me, bye Connor," I heard a few shouts and before we could say anything else he had hung up. Chuckling I looked at Anna,

"Hes a doofus sometimes," Anna smiled,

"You two seem good together and that's just what i saw when he was on the phone," I smiled broadly,

"That means a lot, now before she gets to bored do you want to untack her?" Anna nodded and I led her to the barn noticing that every few moments her hand would go to Flames neck as if making sure she was real.

I smiled as I talked to her and she groomed Flame. They were a good fit, hope fully that would be enough at SCRA.

Chapter 18

"Connor get Wind on the bit!" Callia shouted from where she rode her bay Arabian, Fancy, or independent beauty. We had just gotten back from break a day ago and our instructors had decided that they would switch it up today and sent each team off with a different instructor. Show jumping with Josie for cross country, dressage with Lewis for Show jumping and cross country with Callia for dressage...because let's face it the cross country team is the most free riding of the three.

"Jeremy! Don't let her do that! Keep her in line!" I was remembering now why I decided not to take dressage this year. Callia was known for her hard lessons and her 'take no crap for anyone attitude'.

"No!" I held back a laugh as I saw Ben flash by Star having spooked when he Ben asked for an extended trot. Ben had told me a while ago that she wasn't used to dressage as her family was a more just hit the gas and jump type of riders.

"Ben! Get that horse in line!"

"Sorry!"

"Nick don't think I didn't see that! Let Dante off the bit one more time and I'll ride him!" I swear the whole team gulped. It wasn't as though Callia was a harsh rider it's just when you think of Mamma bear riders that the horses know as 'the one who won't let them get away with anything' you immediately think of Callia and all the things you let your horse get away with flash through your mind and you're suddenly worried about you and your horses sanity.

"Good Jeremy that's lovely, now keep her in that form and transition to a canter," all heads turned to watch as Jeremy transitioned with Venus into a canter. A large sigh of relief was released when Venus held the form her head down on the bit. Although each horse was foaming at the mouth, and both rider and horse were slicked in sweat we had fifteen more minutes of this hour and a half lesson to go. Focusing on my own horse I asked one more time for the bit and this time his head bent in without protest. I frowned, my poor baby boy was to exhausted to protest. Sneaking a pat on his neck I murmured words of encouragement as I to tried for a canter. I sent a quick prayer of thanks as he held it and Callia finally called us to the center.

"Alright that's enough you guys look like you're about to fall off your horses,"

"Whose fault is that?" I choked back a laugh having heard Ben's under his breath comment. If Callia had heard that she'd do something crazy like make him run laps-without star-around the arena.

"Alright go hose your horses off and I suggest you take an ice bath tonight as well," I swear we all shivered just at the thought.

Dismounting of off Wind I awkwardly waddled my way to Nick, my legs jello.

"And I though cross country with no stirrups was hard," Nick gave me a pained expression,

"You're telling me," laughing we made our way to the cross ties and gave Wind and Dante a good rub down before setting them loose of the oats and hay that waited in their stalls. I felt arms drape over me and heard a dramatic groan,

"Remind me never again to doubt your athleticism with cross country!" I laughed at Casey's demand and wrapped an arm around her waist,

"Alright, I give in, I want an ice bath so lets go!" Dragging our feet we somehow made it to our dorms where we pulled on shorts, sports bras and tank tops before heading to the sports facility on campus. It's quite odd you would think the ice baths would be in the locker rooms but instead they were in a sports facility made for ice baths, normal gym equipment and any other shortly needs. Entering we stopped at the front desk and the boy there took one look at us before saying,

"Ice baths are over there," mumbling our thanks we made it to the baths, grabbed a hot chocolate that they were handing out and chose two baths in a corner.

"You first," Casey said nudging me, I shook my head,

"Not happening, you go first,"

"No you!"

"No you" it went on like this for a few minutes before we finally decided to go at the same time. Stripping off our tank tops so we were in our sports bras and shorts we stepped in shivering as we did.

"On three," Casey said as we braced ourselves preparing to sit,

"One"

"Two"

"Three!"

"Ohmygoodness it's so cold!" Sipping my hot cocoa I found some warmth and the ability to feel my toes with the heat of it running through my body though it was quickly extinguished.

"R-r-remind me w-w-w-why we're doing t-t-this?" Casey chartered out,

"S-s-so w-we're n-not sore t-t-tomorrow," Casey sighed and we continued to chatter, drink our hot cocoa and freeze for ten more minutes.

"So cold! So cold!" Casey grumbled as we.buried ourselves in blankets after getting back to the dorm. I nodded in agreement snuggling into Nicks hoodie.

"Some one sick?" I glared at Ben as he walked by, dumb boys and not getting sore.

"Ice bath?" I looked up as my boyfriend entered and nodded. He smiled before sitting down beside me and pulling me onto his lap.

"This better?" I nodded again smiling softly as I snuggled into his chest.

"Seriously? Where's your brother? I need my personal heater," Casey demanded.

"I heard my name?" I laughed as Adam appeared and Casey directed him till they were in a position similar to Nick and I's.

"Oooh we having a cuddle party?" Megan said appearing with Jeremy. She grinned when she saw her own boyfriend, "Ben I want cuddle time!" Ben rolled his eyes before sitting in the comfy chair and pulling Megan onto his lap.

"Dude, this is pretty awkward for me," Jeremy said sitting on the floor. I grinned sweetly at him,

"Oh Jeremy could you turn on the tv? Pretty please?" He rolled his eyes but obliged, turning on secretariat.

"Don't take my baby!" We laughed as Megan shouted at the tv during the coin toss.

"He's not even born yet Meg," I argued, she threw a pillow at me,

"Shut up!"

...

"Hey Hamilton! Can I use my stirrups yet!" We all mentally slapped Ben in the head. It was day to of our changed up lessons and this time we were with Lewis Hamilton, or Hamilton as we called him, he said either that or Mr. Lewis. Obviously we went with Hamilton. And quite obviously he had us do combinations without stirrups which wasn't as much of a problem for me since I rode bareback so often. And then it became a problem when he decided since it seems to easy for me it would be fun to have me, first post Winds bumpy trot which I usually sit without stirrups and then use only my legs to guide him, this includes over jumps.

"Well let's see, since that seems to be getting boring," Hamilton started, "why don't you going Connor in no reins and post Stars trot?" I winced at that. Stars trot was the busiest out of the whole team since Star had the shortest stride.

I choked back a laugh as Ben passed me mumbling,

"I just had to open my big fat mouth didn't I?" Hope Megan was ready for a grumpy boyfriend.

"Good Nick, now Ben lead the group over the three combinations, you and Connor still get no reins," Ben and i sighed in Synch before doing as he said. We made it over the first two before I felt myself start to slide Wind. Trying not to throw him off and stay on at the same time I threw my weight to the opposite side just barely hang on as we flew over the jump and I slowed Wind to a walk before righting myself and getting out of the other way.

"Thank you Connor for not breaking the rules and Ben...Ben do it again without your outside stirrup," the whole team let out a laugh at Ben pointy expression before he did as he was told having as much luck as I did over the jumps.

"Alright, I think that's enough for today, cool down your horses and give them and yourselves a much needed bath," Hamilton dismissed up with a wave of his hands and Ben led the way letting star have. Loose rein as he walked around the arena and we let them walk for about two laps before dismounting and leading our poor foamy horses out to the wash stalls.

"My poor poor legs!" I complained to Nick who had set up beside me after taking both Dante and Winds tack to the tack room. Sometimes it's really handy to have a boyfriend...

"Oh quite complaining and wash your horse!" I rolled my eyes at Ben who was still in a grumpy mood,

"Oh go get a smooch from your girlfriend and stop being grumpy," I quipped back before spraying Wind with his final dose of water.

"There! All done!"

"Really. You just had to didn't you Connor?" I looked around Wind to see Ben standing beside Star and looking as wet as star as well. I started laughing, Jeremy who was across from Ben joined in with Nick after taking in the scene.

"Well hey now your all cooled off!" I sang as Ben gave me a dry look before turning to Nick,

"Nick control your girlfriend," now I glared at him while Nick shook his head,

"You're in for it now Ben," Ben turned just as I threw the rest of my soap water on him dousing him head to toe with out a single dry spot.

"What is going on- oh my gosh Ben you're as wet as Star!" We all broke down as Megan walked in giving her boyfriend an incredulous look before looking at me with the soap bucket and walking over and giving me a high five as we started laughing again.

"Ben Control your girlfriend!" Nick mimicked over the laughter before ducking as Ben threw a sponge at him spoiling Dante,

"Shut i-" Ben was cut off when he started laughing and I looked over to see Dante had whacked Nick with his shopping wet tail and shook out his mane on him. This of course only created more laughter and this time Josie walked in on it,

"How many times do I have to tell you four to get the water on the horse not yourself!" And more laughter as Josie walked away shaking her head saying, "I didn't see anything..."

Eventually we managed to stop laughing enough to dry off our horses and put them in their stalls.

"You are one crazy girl, you know that?" Nick said wrapping his arm around me as we all walked back to the dorm.

I grinned up at him, "yeah but that's why you love me!!" Sneaking out from under his arm I raced ahead and grabbed Megan and pulled her away from Ben before skipping back to the dorm.

Right before we entered she looked at me,

"Good day?" I grinned and nodded,

"Good Day."

Chapter 19

"Everyone ready to go?" Josie asked coming up to Emma, April and I. We were headed out to see the 'prospects' for our advanced teams today and our first stop was in Montana. About a seven hour drive from here and were taking the same fancy vans with the foldout seats that we used for shows to get there. We had decided to leave a three in the morning. Nick, being the sweet boyfriend he was, had woken me up so I wouldn't be late and saw me out of the dorm. The trainers had decided that we should each bring our horses to keep up with our training not to mention each prospect would get to sit in on one of our lessons.

"I'm ready if you guys are!" Emma responded happily. She was the advanced show jumping team captain while April was the advanced Dressage team captain.

"Alright let's get this show on the ride!" We all jumped as Callia came up behind us clapping her hands together. Laughing at our in Synch jump we all loaded into the van. Hamilton in the front with Callia driving while Jose took a back seat with us because Hamilton said,and I quote, ' you are closest to their age and will understand all teenage girl gibberish,'

"I need a window seat! I get carsick!" Emma said diving in ahead of us to get the seat with the biggest window. Laughing at her antics April, Josie and I follow soon after and settle down so Josie is sitting on the single seat across from us while April takes middle between Emma and I. Settling down for the drive ahead didn't curl my legs up to me soon after we unfold the seats giving everyone room to stretch out and elevate their feet. Slipping out my phone I grin when I see a text from Nick.

Nick: you guys head out yet?

Me: Just left

Me: Wish me luck with all this driving time lol

Nick: Alright, good luck ;)

Me: oooh a winky face? That's different

Nick: *sigh* won't you know I'm always evolving

Me: sure whatever rocks your boat

Nick: ...

Nick: Get some sleep

Me: what have we said about telling me to sleep

Nick: ...

Me: ...

Nick: it's been an early morning I think I'm going to catch a few more hours of sleep, text you when I wake up?

Me: you're learning!

Me: of course

Nick: love you to the moon and back

Me: love you to mars and back

Grinning at our cheesiness I turn off my phone and stuff it in my pocket before grabbing the fuzzy blanket I had stuffed In my bag and curling up on the seat quickly drifting off to sleep.

...

tickle

tickle

tickle

I let out a loud sneeze as I rub the sleep out of eyes and sit up to see Emma and April giggling. I roll my eyes when I see a feather in Emma's hands,

"Wow, not even twenty four hours and you two are ganging up on me," at this they burst out into full laughter. Turning I see Josie looking at us with a grin on her face.

"Are we almost there?" Emma asked recovering from her laughter,

"About half an hour till we're at the hotel we're staying at tonight, we're stopping there and dropping off our stuff and changing before heading to the show grounds. Actually since your up I'll go over the prospect that'll be there. These prospect are cross country prospects for advanced. There will also be a show jumper but we're not sure if she'll be enough for advanced," we all nodded seriously as Josie took out a folder.

"Our first cross country prospect is named Charlotte Lewis. She will be a sophomore next year and her horse is a palomino mustang gelding named Crackerjack. So far all I've seen for her information is very fast times. Her horse while not very large is very nimble and fast. He's able to go for long periods of time at the same fast pace. The only fault I've found with them is her horse has a tendency to rush fences but...but somehow that crazy little horse clears them." I laughed, he sounds like a miniature Wind. Josie rolled her eyes at me before continuing,

"Our next cross country prospect is Ava Constantine. She too will be a sophomore next year and is riding a dark bay thoroughbred gelding named Tic Tac. If I remember correctly she isn't one of our top prospects but if anything she'll be a shoo in or intermediate 1 rider. Please keep in mind these riders are already accepted to SCRA and we are just coming to see who will be a good fit for the advanced teams," we all nodded again and she continued, "Ava, while a good rider, tends to let Tic Tac go to much. Unlike Charlotte and CrackerJack Tic Tac will go to much and then refuse if he isn't set up properly. Ava is one that I'm worried relies wholly on a horse and much less on her skills. And finally for Show jumping we have Lola Gordon and her fallen chestnut thoroughbred Rebel Knight. Lola while also a good rider has a tendency to loose focus easily and her horse...well her horse is the same way. And as I said before we think they'll be good prospects for intermediate 1 at least." Josie finished closing her folder.

"We have four shows in total to go to with three riders at each shows except for one which has four and basically it will all be one big circle leading back to SCRA. Any questions?" We all shook our heads no and hear Hamilton shout back at us,

"Alright Ladies we're turning into the hotel now! So quickly check in, change and then get back down here. Don't worry about checking on your horses as I will check on them while you do," we all shouted back out thanks and filed out of the car as it came to a stop. Moving quickly we checked in at the front desk before taking the elevator up to our room. Us three Captains would be sharing while Callia and Josie would be across from us and Hamilton in his own room.

"Nothing I wouldn't give right now to lay down in that bed and take a nap," April groaned as we each changed in similar outfits of breeches, our captain zip up no hood jackets and tall boots. The only difference was I had hunter green breeches and my hair in a braid, Emma, Maroon with her chestnut hair in a pony tail and April, Grey with her red hair loose. Sending a quickly text to Nick to let him know we'd arrived we Moved quickly, grabbing our essentials before filing out into the hall and out to the car after Callia and Josie came out.

"Alright, the shows fifteen minutes from here and as a surprise you all are entered in a show jumping schooling Class! We decided you girls could get used to showing in different disciplines! Yes Emma I know you can show jump." She teased as Emma started to open her mouth, "So each of you will be in at least three shows then at our very last show you can choose your discipline," we all grinned at the news and chatted excitedly as Emma gave us a few tips before we pulled up to the show. Hopping out of the car again I raced around to the trailer while April went through the inside and knocked on the door giving us the ok. Swinging it open I grinned as Wind whinnied at the sigh of me. Letting down the ramp I climbed up and led my gelding out. The others following with their own horses.

"Warren!" I turned and giggled as I saw Emma's fairly small chestnut Holsteiner gelding slobber all over the front of her jacket. Emma rolled her eyes at my giggles and stroked her horses neck.

"I swear out of your crazy gelding Duchess seems calm," April muttered as Wind pranced beside me. I shot her a smile as her black mare tried to go say hello to a passing stallion almost pulling April off her feet.

"Alright girls, follow me to where your horses will be staying tonight. A few stewards are taking your tack there now," grinning happily we follow Hamilton into the barn.

"Alright it's going Warren, Wind then Duchess, April we made sure to request Duchess is put away from any stallions," April rolled her eyes,

"Of course my mare must be boy crazy," she muttered catching a few odd looks from the riders passing by.

One actually winked at April and said, "I hope you are too," causing April's pale face dusted with freckles turn into a tomato. I shot a grin at April who muttered, "shut up," in response before putting Duchess in her stall. Letting Wind loose in his own stall I laughed when I saw Warren lipping at Emma's hair as she tried to get him in the stall when she eventually did the moment she looked at us we burst out laughing.

"Yeah, yeah laugh it up, I'm gonna do the same to you Connor when Winds infamous hot streak comes back," she quipped at me reminding us all of Winds crazy antics. I winced remembering the time when Wind had been awful at coming out of the trailer.

"Alright Ladies our first Prospect, Charlotte Lewis is up on deck so let's get down to the cross course," Hamilton informed us before leading the way to the course. Taking up a sport by one of the harder jumps I heard the announcer,

"Number 658 out of the gate riding Crackerjack," peering down the track I saw a rider come throttling down. It couldn't have been Charlotte as we were rather far out. This rider was riding a familiar looking gelding and he came out strongly against the jump the horses quite obviously well trained muscles rippling as the made the take off point and took off over the jump. They were soon gone and a few riders passed before a palomino gelding came throttling down. Charlotte and Crackerjack, I realised remembering that Josie had said he was a palomino. I grinned as I saw the gelding move sure footed and just when I thought he was going to keep running, maybe even plow through the jump, Charlotte seemed to have given him a question as just as fast as he was moving he took off into a powerful jump for such a small gelding. Letting out a clap as they raced past I grinned at Josie,

"She'd be great on the team. While a little reckless you could tell she works great with that little gelding," I said excitedly and we turned as another right hustled by catching the number I recalled the announcer saying the horse was named Tic Tac so she must be our second cross country prospect. I study the little bit I got out of her run.

"She seems almost not able to control her horse," Emma commented from beside me. I nodded in agreement just because Emma was a show jumper didn't mean she didn't know anything about cross country or even horsemanship.

"Alright guys you've got two hours till the show jumping prospect then your own rounds." Josie informed us, "so you are free to go get food or whatever just be back by 2:15." We all nodded before jogging up to the concessions,

"You guys want to go on a ride after?" Emma asked as we waited in line for hotdogs.

"Yep, I always have to do a walk through on the show grounds with Wind so he doesn't freak," I agreed. Paying quickly for our hotdogs we walked and ate on the way to the stable.

"Well if it ain't Miss boy crazy," We all turn to see the same boy that had winked at April leaning against the wall grinning. April rolled her eyes,

"Oh bug off," the guy seemed to take this as good news and grinned even wider,

"Nah, I think I'm gonna stick around," rolling her eyes once again April walked forward Emma and I soon following.

"Warren!" Emma sing songed as she came up to her geldings stall who stuck his head out and whinnied as his human came up to him,

"Want to go for a ride?" Warren responded by shoving his face against her chest. Emma giggled and stroked his neck before sliding on his halter attached to the lead rope and tied him to one of the bars attached to the stall. Following Emma's lead I entered Winds stall and did the same with his halter and lead.

Grabbing his bridle from the tack box outside his stall I slipped it in place of his halter after giving his a good rub down.

"Want to go for a ride boy?" I whispered into his ear reassuringly, "just you and me," I grin as he laid his head on my shoulder. Stroking him on the neck one last time I lead him out of his stall.

Chapter 20

"Go Anna!" I cheered from the sidelines. We had made it through a total of three shows and we were at the final one that Anna would be reviewed at. Flame was balanced under her beautifully as they entered her head arched in a way that showed her Arabian bloodlines and the power in her movement showing her quarter horse ones.

"She's your friend, right?" Emma asked from beside me as Anna and Flame cantered to the first jump. I nodded grinning and April leaned over joining the conversation,

"If you don't want her for Show jumping Emma I'll take her for Dressage," we all giggled softly at that before turning our attention back to Anna and Flame. Currently they had about three jumps to go and Flame was moving perfectly while Anna directed the fiery mare with ease. Even with the small amount of time they had spent together they already worked well under the saddle out of the saddle though...that was a different story. They flew seamlessly over the final jump,

"And that was Dancing in the Flames ridden by Anna Shires owned by O'Connor Steele," I grinned as a few people looked around obviously recognizing my name. Bouncing out of my seat I jog down the bleachers Emma and April following. The trainers had gone over to the other three riders we had seen go before Anna. Grinning I call over to Anna,

"So I hear you're riding an excellent horse," Anna turned grinning and I tackled her into a hug. "Great job kid, I couldn't have ridden her better myself," I had been facetiming Anna a lot to help them get ready for today over the past few weeks and we had gotten to know each other pretty well.

"Thank you! Are you sure she wasn't to tight on the turn? She's been a little iffy about right turns on her right side," Anna said seriously turning to shut Flames stall door. I laugh at her completely oblivious attitude,

"Anna this is Emma Woods the Show jumping team captain and April Carrillo the Dressage team captain," Anna turned her eyes wide,

"Oh. My. Goodness," Emma grinned and shook hands with Anna,

"It will be a pleasure to have you on the team Anna, don't tell the others but so far I liked your riding style the best," Anna currently looked like she was going to faint and I laughed as Flame bent her head around Anna from inside her stall looking for treats. Anna grinning and stroked Flames Muzzle a little bit pushing her head away, meaning 'don't beg,' Flame obviously insulted by this stomped her hoof and Anna rolled her eyes.

"So Anna, how old is Flame?" April asked starting up a conversation,

"Oh she's...um...five..." both captains looked at her and I nodded smugly, that's right this kid was handling my crazy five year old chestnut mare.

"I thought she was like at least 9," Anna shook her head,

"Flames Connors other mares filly," both captains shot a look at me clearly saying 'why are we even bothering to check her out when you know her so well?'

"Ok, I just got a text from Hamilton," Emma said, "he wants April and I to go talk with the other three prospects and he said, and I quote, 'Tell O'Connor to go take her crazy thoroughbred for a ride as he is currently trying to break out of his stall,'" Emma grins at me while I laugh. The two captains say their goodbyes to Anna and I turn to the girl,

"Want to go take that mare of yours on a ride?" Anna nods and quickly slips Flames bridle on her mares face before following me to Winds stall who, Like Hamilton had said, was trying to break out of his stall. Laughing at my gelding I stroke his face before sliding on his Bridle and leading him out. After giving Anna a leg up I vault onto his back and follow Anna out of the barn and into one of the empty arenas.

"Oh hey! It's boy crazy's friend!" I snort when I see the same guy that had flirted with April at the first show in Montana leaning on the wall by the gate.

"Boy crazies gone down to concessions if you want to catch her," I replied with a smirk. His grin widens and he jogs away. Anna gives me a curious look,

"Who was that?"

"At the first show April said 'why is my mare boy crazy?' And he happened to walk by and hear her." I snorted at the memory, "he then said 'hope you are go's with a wink. He flirted with her the whole time we were at the show. Good thing he's pretty good looking or April probably would've set her mare on him," Anna chuckled at my explanation,

"Well sounds like it's been an eventful week," I

I nodded, "that's for sure, Nick is going crazy though, said the cross country team has been running the same exercise for the whole week cuz the rider I left in charge, Ben, couldn't think of anything else," I tapped my chin thoughtfully, "now that I think about it I have no idea why I left him in charge," I snapped my fingers, "oh that's right I couldn't play favorites with my boyfriend and with Ally and Lukas no longer training there since they are leaving, then there was only Ben and Jeremy and while Jeremy is cool and all he's also a freshman," I explained mostly to myself.

"You know...Jeremy is pretty good looking..." I continued casting Anna, who was completely oblivious, a sly look.

"Thats cool...I guess?" Anna relied shrugging her shoulders.

I rolled my eyes, "you have much to learn my child..." I sighed dramatically,

"Now let's go over some jumps!"

...

"Remind me why I am around you two?" I grumbled glaring as April and Emma once again wake me up from my nap on our ten our car ride back to school.

"Because you have too and because you love us!" Emma sang while April smirked at me. Surprisingly Emma is a year older then both April and I.

"Who wants food?" Callia shouted back from the front seat. An immediate answer of three 'me's is the response.

"Alright we're pulling up to a McDonald's what's the orders?"

"Big Mac, medium fries, and medium sprite," April shouted, then Emma,

"12 chicken nuggets, large fries, and chocolate shake," and finally me,

"Big Mac, large fries, and chocolate shake!" I get there stares no doubt because my order is the largest.

"I slept through lunch ok, and the one time you didn't wake me up I didn't get any food!" I complained.

They both started chuckling at me before grabbing the food that was soon handed back to us after ordering.

...

"So out two have squeezed all the relationship info out of me but what about you two?" I question chewing on a fry. The two had taken to getting all the details on Nick and I's relationship so now I was determined to get my own details on their relationships. Almost immediately Emma's face turned red. I pounced,

"Who is he?"

"W-what?" I roll my eyes and keep poking,

"Tell meeee!" Emma sighed before relenting

"His names Zach," I grinned,

"Are you two together?" She shrugged

"Whats that supposed to mean?" April piped up,

"He kissed me but...um hasn't said anything since," I exchange a look with April. She grabbed Emma and held her down while just grabbed her phone which sat next to her,

"CONNOR DON'T DARE!!!" Emma shouted while I quickly scrolled through her contacts and clicked on the call button for the contact that was named Zach

"Emma?" I grinned, jackpot.

"Hi is this Zach?" I asked sweetly,

"Um...Who is this?"

"Oh well this is Connor Emma's friend,"

"Uh huh,"

"Anyways I was wondering how you felt about my dear friend?"

"..."

"You still there?"

"Emma's an amazing person and she is far to good for this world,"

"Oh...is that so?" I grinned as Emma glared at me,

"Well...yeah,"

"So I mean obviously she needs a boyfriend to protect her from the world right," I mentally sighed at my words, not my best...I'll admit that.

"I mean...I guess,"

"Mhm, and you'd like to be that person,"

"Yeah," I did a happy dance at his response,

"You and Emma will have a lot to talk about. We get back in two hours so be at the courtyard by barn six in two hours!" I sang

"Ok,"

"Bye now," hanging up I cheer happily and April finally let's a fuming Emma up and I toss Emma her phone.

"He's meeting you when you get back," Emma's face immediately turned beet red as she stares down at her phone,

"I'm never letting you near my phone again," she muttered shoving it under she thigh. I grinned before settling back in my seat and finishing off my fries.

"Admit it, you love me,"

"Mhm sure," Emma grumbled sarcastically before smiling a bit.

"I'm cupid!" I exclaimed while I basically heard everyone in the car roll their eyes.

...

"Connor!" I whirled around and dropped my duffel before launching into Nicks outstretched arms. Twirling me around he set me down and not a moment later pressed a kiss to my lips.

"Get a room you two!" I pull away from Nick to glare at Emma who was laughing. Little did she know I saw a boy coming up beside her with families with r ease.

"Oh! You must be Zachary!" Emma's face was soon a tomato as she looked at him.

"Oh...Uh...hey...Uh...Zach," Zach grinned,

"Mind if I walk you back to your dorm?" We had already put away our horses so she no excuse,

"Um sure...I uh....just need to get my bag," Emma said before a bag was thrown at her by April. Emma glared at the other captain before walking away with a wave. I grinned as I saw Zach extend his arm around her shoulders not long after.

"I AM CUPID!" I shouted getting a few curious looks until Nick covered my mouth and shouldered my duffel leading me back to the dorm with a few muttered apologies to the trainers.

"Connie!" The moment we entered the dorm building I was tackled by my friends in an instant.

"Never leave us with these knuckleheads again!" Casey and Megan shouted at once while their boyfriends rolled their eyes and let go on my letting my two best friends hug the life out of me.

"Let me get right on that," I said sarcastically as I found I couldn't move, "I mean it's not like I can move right now anyways," they let go and started rambling about all the boys had done.

"Bennykins!" I yelled seeing Ben try to sneak away. Running at him I launched myself onto his back. After Will had left I had found Ben like the others in our dorm had become my best friend.

"Good to see you to Connor!" he laughed before I dropped off his back grinning.

"You it sure is, now where's my child!" I shouted looking for Jeremy.

"Hes out on a hack," Casey explained leaning on Adam. I glare at the floor and walk to the living room grumbling

"Ok, who wants a movie?" Adam asked following me with Casey and the others.

"War Horse!" I shouted falling onto the love seat. My legs were soon picked up and placed on Nicks lap as he sat down beside me. Nods went around the room as everyone agreed and Adam popped in the movie. Flipping around so my head was on Nicks lap I snuggled into him as he threw a throw blanket over me.

"Anyone home?" I shot into sitting position as Jeremy entered and crossed my arms glaring.

"And where were you young man?" Jeremy seemed shocked by my attitude until I held out my arms for a hug, "now come hug me y child!" Jeremy laughed doing as he was told before settling onto the floor beside Ben. I grinned before falling back onto Nicks lap. I looked around the room as my friends shouted at the tv. My friends were awesome. I thought. But no, my friends aren't just my friends they had become my family.

Chapter 21

"Good you guys, you're looking great!" Josie called from the center of the arena as we cantered over the small course.O nly one week of school remained and we were at our final lessons of the season."Alright guys bring it in!" Slowing Wind to a walk I directed him in between Ben and Nick."This has been an amazing season you guys and I cannot wait for next year," Josie gushed clapping her hands together, "as you know next year is going to be very different but I have every ounce of confidence that you guys will do amazing!" I grinned as Ben let out a whoop, he always got how we were feeling right."Now one final time this year at school go cool off your horses and give them a well deserved rest!" Grinning I directed Wind our to the rail at a walk and took my feet out of the stirrups sighing at the sense of relief."You ready to go home?" Nick asked coming up beside me on Dante. "Yeah, I think I am," I said sadly knowing that I wouldn't get to see him everyday like at school."How's Anna coming along?" He questioned grabbing my hand off of my thigh where it rested."Great, I really think she and Flame are gonna rock the show world," I admitted proudly,"Ok quit with the mushiness you two!" Ben called from behind us, star shaking his head in agreement.

"You're one to talk Ben! Were you or were you not making out with Megan on the couch yesterday!" I teased laughing as Ben's cheeks and ears turned bright red.

"Oooh Ben's getting some!" Jeremy quipped causing us all to break out in laughter.

"Jerks," Ben mumbled pulling Star to a stop and hopping off.

"Take it back! You know you love us!" I said shaking a fist at him as I pulled Wind to a stop as well.

"Do I though? Do I really?" I rolled my eyes as Ben's dramatic ways. Shoving his shoulder as we walk out of the arena the others following.

"So my dear child," I started clipping wind into the cross ties.

Jeremy cast me an odd look, "what this time?"

"As you know Anna is your age and will be coming here next year, so..." I paused lifting Winds saddle off his back,

"I know this is kinda weird to ask but the girls been through a lot, could you keep an eye on here? I mean I'm not asking for you to babysit her or pretend to be her friend or anything just keep an eye on her make sure she's ok every once in awhile," I rambled scurrying Winds back.

"Connor," Jeremy said cutting me off, "Anna sound like a wonderful equestrian and I was hoping to get to know her at least a little bit," I grinned at this mentally constructing a plan. Shrugging Winds bridle onto my shoulder I nodded to Jeremy before lugging my tack to my tack locker. Locking it all up I headed back to Wind only to find Nick standing at his head chatting with Jeremy as he stroked Wind. Grinning I walked up to him from behind and wrapped my arms around his waist.

Nick lifted his arm cleaning his head to look at me,

"Piggy back ride?" I asked, Nick rolled his eyes and squared down as I released him, allowing me to hop on his back. Laughing as Wind nudged me as if to ask, 'how'd you get so tall?'holding onto Nick with one hand I managed to clip Wind lead on his halter and release him from the cross ties before rest my head on Nicks shoulder. Nick turned his head giving me a soft kiss on the temple before carrying me to Wind stall where I Jumped of his back long enough to put Wind away before jumping back on.

Sighing in content as Nick carried me easily back to the dorm I closed my eyes resting my head on his shoulder again. Not opening my eyes as we entered the dorm and Nick carried me up the stairs I only opened them when we were at my dorm. Smiling softly at Nick I hopped off his back and led him into my dorm. Grabbing a grey Capri sweats, and a black cami I ducked into the bathroom and changed quickly out of my riding clothes. Tying my hair up into a bun before leaving the bathroom and climbing up my beds ladder to where Nick was lying, his shoes discarded on the floor by the door.

Cuddling into his side I laid my head on his chest listening to the sound of his breathing as he wrapped an arm around my waist.

"I don't think I want school to end," I mumbled,

"Look at it this way, we'll be back in at least three months," he replied pressing a kiss to my hair line. Yawning I snuggled closer breathing in his piney smell.

"I love you Connor, so so much," he murmured into my hair.

"I love you too Nick,"

...

"Wake up lovebirds!" I yawned opening my eyes as Megan barged into Casey and I's dorm room yelling at Nick and I.

"Don't make me count from three!" She warned and I walked Nick in the cheek waking him up enough that he removed his iron like grip from my waist and allowed me to sit up. Yawning again I climbed down the ladder Nick soon following yawning and rubbing his eyes on the ground his hair messed up in a way that made him look even cuter.

"Finlly!" I rolled my eyes at Megan's dramatics and untied my hair from its bun.

"Casey and I want to go on a night ride so let's go!" She said ushering me into my bathroom and Nick out of my dorm and probably so he wouldn't keep me any longer. Sighing I grabbed a pair of Ariat Maroon full seat Ice fil breeches and a grey long sleeve seeing as the sun was already close to being gone at this time of day no longer shinning brightly through the blinds of the single window in our bathroom. Yes I know it is rather odd to have a window in a dorm bathroom.

Changing quickly I braided my hair into a loose braid and grabbed my hat before slipping on a pair of Zocks and my paddock boots and

Half chaps over them. Exiting the bathroom I jogged down the stairs not bothering to wait for any one. A pit building in my stomach. I didn't know why but I needed to see my baby and I needed to see him now. Not bothering to grab my phone I broke into a dead run once outside of the dorm and towards the barn. I'd learned early long that whenever I get a bad feeling in my stomach to check on my horse.

"Wind!" I called as I entered the barn. No answer only the sound of pacing hoof steps and hay being trodden under hoof.

Rising to his stall I found my beautiful boy drenched in sweat foam frothing at the mouth as he tried to lay down.

"No, no, no!" I muttered rushing into his stall and pushing against him as much as I could struggling to keep him standing.

"Come on bud stay standing!" I murmured to him as I grabbed his halter and lead, slipping it on before leading him out of the stall. From what I had heard about colic as I was lucky enough not to have experienced a horse with it before it was best to keep him moving and not letting him lay down or roll.

"Keep walking Wind just keep moving, please my beautiful boy, please," I begged as he struggled to walk next to me leaning weight onto me and I struggled to hold him up.

"Connor? What's going on?" Casey's worried face appeared with Megan at her side seeing my state with Wind was probably not a good one.

"H-he's colicking," I shuddered out struggling to keep him walking or even standing.

"Megan, get Adam!" Casey instructed rushing beside Wind only for him to stop his hoof raising his head wildly as she approached. I knew that sign.

"Casey stay back!" I warned. When Wind was injured, not feeling well or even just in a bad mood he hated for others to come near him, he used to hate it for me to come near him but now he had accepted me but it seemed at this point only me.

Casey did as I said,

"Can you get the school vet?" Casey shook her head,

"The Vet had to go down to a stable about an hour away who had an emergency with one of their pregnant mares," I felt my eyes tearing up, no no no this couldn't happen.

"Come on Wind keep moving! Please my beautiful boy keep moving!" I murmured as Wind snorted but did as I said moving with me resting his own shoulder on mine.

"Connor!" I choked back tears in relief as Adam appeared his new vet bag in hand.

"Colic," I said looked at him knowing I looked even worse now with my puffy eyes and blotchy cheeks. Adam nodded seriously moving with purposeful steps just as Ben, Jeremy and Nick arrived.

"Wait," I said stopping Adam from moving as Winds eyes started flash,

"Nick, Ben, Jeremy I need you to help hold him steady or he won't let anyone else near him," Adam nodded again and the other moved forward as I held Winds head steady.

"Easy boy, they're gonna help you, easy now," I murmured to him as Nick came up on the other side bracing himself against Winds shoulder and holding a part of his bridle as well.

Ben and Jeremy on the other hand clasped hands behind his hid legs and pretty soon we were all bracing him and holding him steady as he tried to move away. Adam nodded to us all taking out his stethoscope and putting it against his stomach for a moment before running his hands along the stomach.

"Its definitely Colic, we need to get him to the clinic there's not much I can do, I haven't handled this before," Adam admitted. I nodded tears filling my eyes as Adam sent Megan to get Josie.

"What in the name of Sam's hill is going on here?" I looked away from Wind for only a moment to glance and see the headmistress who I'd only met once and seen a few times at assemblies standing in the door way.

"Colic," Nick explained. Ms. Walker nodded before taking out her phone and quickly typing in a number,

"Dr. Frederick we have a horse with colic and are about to be on our way to your clinic," she stated letting the vet speak for a moment before she hung up."Alright I'm having a trailer pulled around. There is a vet clinic about half an hour away." She informed us typing into he phone. A few moments later we heard the rumbling of a truck and trailer. I led Wind out of the barn to see Josie and Megan hop out running to the trailer for to open it. "Easy boy it'll be ok," I murmured to Wind leading him slowly into the trailer."Are you going to ride with him?" Josie asked as I tied him in,"Yeah," I replied numbly stroking Winds neck. Josie swing the door shut and I heard footsteps as she ran around to the truck and the rumbling as the truck started up. Bracing myself against the trailer wall and Wind I continued murmuring words of comfort him."It'll be okay but it'll all be ok,"

Chapter 22

"As you already figured out it is colic luckily it was caught early on," Dr. Fredrick confirmed as we stood in the waiting area of the clinic. Nicks arm wrapped around my waist as I leaned into him fatigue from the night finally setting in. "And since we caught it early on there wasn't a need for a surgery and Running Wind will be ok. We would like to keep him overnight for observation but there shouldn't be any problems for him to go back tomorrow afternoon." I sighed in relief as Dr. Fredrick finished."Can I see him?" I asked straightening up. Dr. Fredrick nodded and Nick released me to follow Dr. Fredrick down the hall. Walking quickly I nearly cried in relief when I saw Wind standing ears perked, head rising slowly as I arrived at his stall. Not bothering to ask I moved into his stall quickly throwing my arms around his neck and burying my face into his mane."Oh Wind, don't you dare do that ever again," I murmured inhaling his sweet smell."Connor?" I lifted my head only for a moment to see Adam standing outside the stall. He frowned his eyes asking the unsaid question, do you need anything?"I'm staying here until he leaves," I stated softly not leaving it up for discussion,"I'll talk to Dr. Fredrick," was all he said before I head his footsteps fade away.I smiled softly as Wind curled his head around so it rested over my back pulling me into a horse hug. Rubbing the soft spot behind his ears I grinned wider when I heard him sigh almost as though all the tension was leaving his body. Eventually I released him from the hug and settled down on the ground leaning against the wall as Wind closed closed his eyes head drooping low as he fell asleep. Relaxing for the first time since last night I closed my own eyes and slowly nodded off to sleep....When I woke I found Nick sitting beside me, his arm wrapped around me his own eyes open and watching Wind who was looking around much more alert then when I first saw him earlier.

"Morning beautiful," I have Nick a sleepy smile burrowing deeper into his side," you practically slept through the day, Wind is being released in a bjt and you need to get packing. You go home tomorrow," he informed me. I sighed not bothering to move, packing could wait.

"Ms.Steele?" I looked up to see a Vet tech looking over the stall door, "it's time to get Running Wind ready to go," I smiled softly and stood stretching before accepting the halter and lead Nick handed me. Slipping it on Wind, I opened the stall door and less him out. Happy to see him standing strongly.

"Ms. Steele, we recommend the running Wind be kept on stall rest for at least a week and is brought back into work not to suddenly," the Vet tech informed me as we walked to the SCRA trailer waiting outside. I was happy to find Josie and Adam standing by the open trailer door. Leading Wind up the ramp slowly I tied him in and hopped out quickly moving around to the truck after Adam latched the door and ramp shut. Waving to the vet tech as Adam hopped in the front seat while Nick took the seat next to me.

"Alright let's get you guys back," Josie said as she pulls d outbound the clinic parking lot and onto the road. Leaning my head on Nicks shoulder I smiled softly as I watched Josie and Adam squabble over the radio. I was going to miss this so much. As we drove back to the school yet again I slowly nodded off to sleep."Connor we're here," sitting up slowly I rubbed my eyed and unbuckled my seat belt before sliding out of the truck after Nick.Jogging around back to the trailer as Josie swung it open I slipped inside to get wind. Sighing when I saw Wind looking around and when he saw me letting out a low nicker. Grinning I untied his lead and slowly led him out of the trailer and to the barn. Letting him into his stall I quickly hung up him halter and lead before returning my attention to him but am soon interrupted by Adam who starts pushing me out of the stable."Wind will be fine if he is left alone for a bit but you on the other hand will be strangled by our parents tomorrow if you aren't packed." I started to object but Abadan just sighs and in one smooth move throws me over his shoulder."Adam! Let me down!!" I complained slapping him on the back. My head jerked up when I felt Adam slap me on the butt."Cool it Lil sis," I rolled my eyes and stopped fighting him as we entered the dorm and I got some weird looks from our friends who just shook their heads. Adam slowly climbed the stairs and dropped me at my door only for me to be grabbed and pulled into Casey and I's dorm room by Casey."Finally!" Casey exclaimed throwing a suitcase at me,"Get packing! It's four in the afternoon! You have to be packed and ready to go by 11 am tomorrow and the final dorm ride is in two hours," I sighed in response," you know I can't ride Wind right?" Casey grinned,"That's why your doubling with Me! You can't get around this!" She said tanking open my drawers and neatly packing some of my clothes into a suitcase while I got up and packed the one she had given me with all but one pair of riding clothes for tomorrow. It actually didn't take us that long to pack all of my things as the most things o had were pictures and riding clothes."Ladies we're leaving in ten!" Adam called through our door causing me to jump up from where I sat packing the final bit of my clothes. "Alright we'll be down in a minute!" Casey called back from on top of a chair where she was taking down the last of our shared posters. Sighing we both took another look around the room sad that it seemed so empty now. Linking elbows we exited our dorm and jogged down the stair to meet the others before we all headed to the barn. Seeing that everyone was there when we got there we all headed out to the barn separating once their to each horse. Saying a hello to Wind with a kiss on his nose I walked over to where Casey was sliding a western no brow band bridle in Camelot who stood by patiently. Grinning at me she led Camelot out of his stall and mounted onto his bareback before offering a hand down to me. Grabbing her hand I pulled myself up and we waited by the entrance as the other mounted up almost all of them with their western saddles. Grinning as Adam and Nick came up besides us Casey kicked Camelot in the flanks going at a flat out gallop as we heard the guys and Megan complaining behind us. Grinning as I held onto my best friend I close my eyes and just enjoyed the feel of the wind in my hair and hoof beats beneath me."Woah Cam woah," I heard Casey call as she slowed Camelot and he started to prance beneath us.Eventually Camelot slowed to a walk and soon enough the other caught up,"Really you two? You had to leave me with the boys?" Megan complained rousing a few objections from the guys."Alright Alright, how about we continue the ride?" Jeremy calmed us waving forward Casey and I as he fell in beside us with the others following."In all fairness I totally won that race," Jeremy whispered over to us loud enough for the others to hear,"On your dreams freshman!!" Adam called from the back next to Nick who calmly patted Dante,"Wanna bet Steele?" Jeremy taunted grinning as Adam glared realizing there was no way for him to reach Jeremy at this moment,"One day, one day," he muttered causing me to laugh."Hey you guys want to canter?" I asked getting a unanimous yes. Laughing I held onto Casey and she yet again urged Camelot forward only this time into a canter. Grinning as the palomino moved smoothly beneath us his step never faltering as Casey urged him forward. This was how you could tell a rose trusted his rider. When he moved forward to where his rider wanted without question.Eventually we came up to the steepest part of down hill in the trail that required a walk. Leaning back as Casey slowed Camelot we made our way down the trail single file. Grinning as we hit the end and Camelot instantly went back into a canter only this time uphill and toward the top of the trail where the best view of the academy was. We came to a stop the other lining up beside us as we looked out over the academy. I smiled as I saw my friends match my own feelings on their faces. Even if we were going home tomorrow a part of our hearts would always remain at the academy. To much had happened here for it not to. Besides we were Stone Creek riding academy riders.

CPSIA information can be obtained
at www.ICGtesting.com
Printed in the USA
LVHW021002211122
733502LV00008B/519